AMBER'S SECRET

AMBER'S SECRET

Ann Pilling

Illustrated by Victor Ambrus

An imprint of HarperCollins*Publishers*

Other titles by Ann Pilling:

The Empty Frame
Black Harvest
The Pit
The Witch of Lagg
The Beggar's Curse

First published in Great Britain by Collins 2000
Collins is an imprint of HarperCollins*Publishers* Ltd
77-85 Fulham Palace Road, Hammersmith,
London, W6 8JB

The HarperCollins website address is:
www.**fire**and**water**.com

3 5 7 9 8 6 4 2

Text copyright © Ann Pilling 2000
Illustrations copyright © Victor Ambrus 2000

ISBN 0 00 675469 4

The author and illustrator assert the moral right to be
identified as the author and illustrator of the work.

Printed and bound in Great Britain by
Omnia Books Limited, Glasgow

for my grandson
Francesco Joseph
and for his great grandmother
Elizabeth Irene

Things men have made with wakened hands, and put
  soft life into
are awake through years with transferred touch, and go
  on glowing
for long years.
And for this reason, some old things are lovely
warm still with the life of forgotten men who made
them.

D H Lawrence

1

'Did you know,' said Amber one day to her friend Sally, 'that if you pick up the phone and ring Appleford 616 you can talk to God?'

Sally stared. Amber was a gypsy child, she knew secrets. She knew the place on Furze Hill where rabbits came to graze in the afternoon. She knew where the kingfisher lived at Tolly Reach. She could ride her pony bareback across the fields. If anyone knew about talking to God it would be Amber.

But there was something uncertain about her, something vanishing. She only came to school when the Fair was in town, at Christmas time, and in the summer. Sally would have liked Amber to be her very best friend but she was always going away.

They were sitting by the stream at the end of the

allotments. It was by this stream that they had their most important talks. Sally stared at the water. Then she said, 'Have you tried it?' She needed to talk to someone like God very much, or to an angel, or to some helpful human being who might know what to do. Something terrible had happened at home.

'Oh *no*,' said Amber. 'It's only for emergencies.'

Sally was disappointed. She thought for a little while then she said, 'You mean like 999? You mean like Police, Fire, Ambulance?'

'Sort of. But it's a lot more special.'

'Will you write that number down for me?' said Sally.

But Amber scrunched her lips again. She looked as if she was going to say 'no' and the trouble was that Sally forgot things. 'Scatterbrain Sally' was what her mother called her.

'*Please*,' she whispered. As she waited, the terrible thing at home became ten times more terrible.

'What will you give me if I do?' said Amber.

This was the one bit of Amber that Sally didn't like, the bit that made bargains. She felt in her pockets while Amber watched very carefully, her glossy black head moving now this way, now that, like a bird.

On to the bank Sally put two sweets, a piece of blue string and a rubber shaped like a frog. Then she found a stub of pencil and laid it beside the rest. Amber inspected everything.

'Is that all?' she demanded.

'That's all... today,' Sally said slowly, as if, on normal days, her pockets were stuffed with treasures.

Amber swept everything except the pencil into the brilliant patchwork bag she brought to school with her things in. Then she picked up the pencil stub and wrote down the number on Sally's hand.

'Ouch!' squeaked Sally. Amber was pressing much too hard.

'Pencil's not much good on skin,' said Amber. 'I've got to press.'

When she had finished, Sally inspected her hand. 'I can't really see it,' she told Amber nervously. 'Could you write it on some paper?'

'Haven't got any paper,' Amber said. She sounded grumpy now. She wrapped her long sunburnt arms round her knees and stared moodily into the slow brown water. Her little gold earrings glinted in the sun and her rainbow-coloured dress was like bright feathers. Sally, who had thick blonde plaits and short stubby legs, felt boring and plain next to Amber, plain as bread.

She said, 'I'll get some paper. Wait here.' And she ran off up the path that went through the middle of the allotments. When she reached the place where they made bonfires she rummaged about among the rusty oil drums. Very soon she soon found a brown paper bag, the kind one of the old men might have brought, with his sandwiches in. A lot of quite old people came to grow things on the allotments, and stayed the whole day.

'Will this do?' asked Sally, holding it out to Amber.

Amber inspected the greasy bag, tore a piece off the corner and scribbled down the number. But she still seemed cross. It was as if giving Sally the important number was like telling somebody your name for the very first time, as if it gave that somebody a kind of power over you.

'There you are, Sally Bell,' she said, slapping the scrap of brown paper into Sally's hand, and the next minute she was gone, running very fast along the path towards Tolly Reach where the kingfisher was and where, across the fields, in a lay-by on the main road, the gypsies had their caravans.

'*Sally Bell*'. That didn't feel very friendly. Sally called Amber 'Amber'. If the gypsy girl had another name then nobody knew it; it was one of the magic things about her.

Sally walked home looking at the faint writing on the palm of her hand. From time to time she felt inside her pocket for the tiny scrap of brown paper. She must put it in a very safe place. It was a good thing she had that paper because she couldn't memorise the number. In the place where other people had a memory, Sally had a 'forgettery', that's what her mum said.

As she lay in bed that night she discovered that the bath water had washed the faint pencil marks quite off her hand. But hanging over a chair was her blue cotton frock with the deep pockets and in the left-hand pocket was Amber's special number. The thought of it comforted her as she drifted off to sleep. It was like a warm hot water bottle held against her tummy. It promised help, help to sort out the terrible thing.

2

The terrible thing hadn't happened in the house in which Sally had gone to bed. She was sleeping at 'Next Door's', where Mrs Spinks lived. Mrs Spinks was looking after her because her mother was in hospital.

This was awful for Sally but it wasn't the terrible thing. The doctor had told Mrs Spinks and Mrs Spinks had told her that Mum would get better soon. So Sally tried not to worry and it was all right until the day she went to the hospital and wasn't allowed to see her mother because they had put her in a special room for very ill people.

After that, Sally worried very much indeed and she asked Mrs Spinks to write to her father straight away, or even to send him a telegram, to Abroad where he was working. But Mrs Spinks said no, not yet anyway. It was Abroad where Mum had caught the illness, when she last visited Dad.

Mrs Spinks said that she had her instructions from Mum. These were that Dad mustn't be told about the illness because it would only worry him, and besides, she really was going to be *all right*. The doctor had said so. Sally tried and tried to believe Mrs Spinks but she didn't succeed. Why had they put Mum into that special room if she was going to be 'all right'? When she'd said this to Mrs Spinks, she'd just turned her thin old-lady lips into a single line. That meant 'No more questions, Sally Bell'.

Her big brother, Alan, suddenly going away with the army, to do his National Service, wasn't the terrible thing either, though if he hadn't gone, they could have stayed together in their own house, till Mum came back. Alan was good at looking after Sally. But he'd said, 'When a soldier gets his orders, Sally Bell, he has to obey. It's like school.' It was funny how Alan called her 'Sally Bell', like Amber and Mrs Spinks; but he didn't do it in a grumpy way.

No, the terrible thing had happened the day before Sally had slept her first night Next Door at Mrs Spinks's. It had happened when she was all alone in their own house. It had happened in the hall.

She'd borrowed the key from where Mrs Spinks kept it, under a red plant pot on her kitchen windowsill, and gone home to feed William her pet mouse. Mrs Spinks didn't like mice, not even clean white ones who lived in clean cages. So William had to stay behind.

Sally had made him a promise. While she was at Mrs Spinks's she would come and see him every day, and give him a run around. What nobody knew was that Sally often gave him quite big runs around, when no-one was looking. He knew Sally's voice and he always came back to his cage. He was a brilliant mouse.

But that day, William seemed to be in a mood. He wouldn't even come out when Sally opened his cage, he just sulked in a corner. When she put her finger inside and made wheedling noises he disappeared into a cocoon of straw. She knew what was wrong. William was sensitive. Sally was sad so he was being sad too.

She sat in the middle of the carpet and looked round the big square hall. Its walls were covered with the carved wooden masks of animal-people and bird-people which Dad had brought home from Abroad. The house itself felt sad, as if it knew they had all gone away and left it. Even the grandfather clock had stopped ticking.

Mum loved the old clock. It had belonged to her mum's mum's dad. Nobody touched it but Mum because she said she knew its little ways. 'Look after Grandfather for me, Sally,' Mum had said, when she went off to the hospital. But now even Grandfather had fallen silent. Something felt very bad indeed.

Sally decided to wind the clock up. She knew exactly how to do it and where Mum kept the key. She had a feeling that if Grandfather started ticking again, Mum might start getting better. Sally sometimes got these funny feelings but she didn't tell anybody about them. She just did what they advised.

To Sally, the old clock felt more like a person than a piece of furniture, and she knew a lot about Grandfather because, once, a man had come to clean him. The week he came their class had been doing a school project on 'Time', so she'd asked him a lot of questions and written down all the answers. Her project had ended up being all about their very own grandfather clock and she had been given a gold star for it.

She had discovered, for example, that when the clock was made, in the olden days, it had been made in three different parts which all fitted nicely together. There was a bottom part, which stood firmly on the floor and held everything else up, and into this slid 'the trunk', which had a door in it. You could open the door and see the huge weights and the pendulum swinging to and fro. On top of the trunk was a carved case which held the painted face and the shining brass hands and, hidden behind all this, the actual works of the clock, the most important part. This wooden case also slid on and off and it was called the 'hood'.

When Mum and Dad read Sally's project, and admired the gold star, they said that she knew more about the old clock than anybody.

Sally fetched the key and the stool Mum stood on, when she wound Grandfather. But she was much shorter than her mother and she couldn't reach the keyholes in the face of the clock. So she put the key into her pocket and went into the study where Dad kept all his books.

She found four enormous ones on the bottom shelf. They were so huge and heavy that she had to carry them into the hall one by one. With the books, she made a neat platform and on to this she put the stool. Then, very carefully, she climbed up. The stool wobbled a bit so Sally did everything slowly, to keep her balance.

She still couldn't reach the holes so she went back to Dad's bookshelves and fetched four more books. It was quite a tall platform now and the stool felt more wobbly. But Sally was determined to get Grandfather ticking again.

Very carefully, and holding on to the clock very tight with her left hand, Sally opened the glass door that protected the face. She had never been so close to Grandfather before. Now she could see that the little girls painted in each corner had pretty, rosy faces. From down below they had looked like little blobs.

One had a fur coat on, she was Winter. One was picking daffodils, she was Spring. One stood in the middle of a field of golden corn, and was Summer. One held a basket of apples, and was Autumn. In between Winter and Spring there was a moon with a big, kindly face, a moon that moved slowly out of sight as the days ticked by, and changed into the sun. Underneath were some numbers that also changed and, under them, the months of the year. And she could see now that the clock had stopped on the second day of July, the day that Mum had been taken into hospital. Sally stared at the face of the clock and felt like crying.

Just as she took the key out of her pocket, something unexpected happened. William must have crept out of his cocoon of straw and come to see what she was doing. Suddenly, without any warning, he ran straight up the clock, his tiny pink feet scurrying along her bare arm and up her fingers. When he reached the very top he sat on one of the carved wooden roses that decorated the case, staring down at her cheekily, his beautiful whiskers all of a quiver.

The feel of his cold little feet on her skin was such a shock that Sally jumped violently, started to sway, and then to wobble. She knew she mustn't panic so she stayed exactly where she was until she got her balance again. She was cross with William, so she ignored him.

Carefully, Sally inserted the big old key in to the

left-hand winding hole and began to turn it. The clock made gentle creaking noises and there was a dull thudding from inside. She knew that it was the sound of the huge weight banging against the door as it travelled up to the top on its thin, strong thread. When she stopped winding, the clock struck three times. Sally was excited. That meant the striking part of Grandfather was properly wound up again.

But now she had to wind up the part which moved the hands round, and told you the time, so she put the key into the right-hand winding hole.

From on top of the clock, William gave a pitiful little squeak. He wanted to come down again. He liked playing in Sally's hair, he liked making nests in it. Sally looked up. 'You'll just have to wait,' she said firmly. 'I'm concentrating on this.'

But William took no notice. He had discovered that it was much easier to run up things than to slither down them and Sally's nice thick hair spelt safety. To William it was like the safety blanket held out by firemen for someone stuck on the top of a burning building. He bunched himself up into a tight white ball and took an almighty leap.

'What the— oh no— help…!' The shock of William landing on her head sent Sally grabbing at the clock. She dropped the key and the stool tipped over and crashed on to the floor and she was left hanging on to the clock by her fingertips, clutching at the polished wooden columns that held up the beautifully carved face. She could hear both the weights bumping about very heavily and now Grandfather seemed to have come to life. He had started to move forwards with a terrifying, lurching motion.

There was a strange scraping noise, like a big, obstinate rusty nail being pulled out of something, and the clock was coming away from the wall – it was falling over! It had been screwed to the wall by Dad, but now—

Sally screamed, threw herself to one side, and landed in a heap on the far side of the hall as the clock toppled right over and hit the floor with the most enormous crash, followed by all kinds of weird noises. As she lay on the carpet, quite unable to move for shock and terror, there was a chinking noise, then a lot of funny bonging sounds, then the steady tinkle of glass.

Then, after all the noises, an awful silence fell. Sally shut her eyes tight, she didn't want to look. But as she lay on the carpet she could hear wheezy, creaky sounds coming from the direction of the clock. It was like a very old person settling down to sleep.

She listened, thinking about Grandfather Bell, who had lived until he was one hundred and one years old. Grandfather Clock was even older, and the thing Mum loved best after Dad, Alan and Sally.

At last, she made herself get up from the carpet. She made herself walk across the hall. She made herself look at the clock. And when Sally saw what had happened, she really did burst into tears and once she had started to cry she felt she would never stop.

Grandfather's 'trunk', the case that held the pendulum and the weights, had split into two pieces. The wooden columns which had risen up on each side of the glass door, holding up the roof of the clock with its two wooden roses, and its pointy carvings, were broken into tiny little bits, and all the other carvings seemed to have vanished completely. It was as if some evil magician had waved a magic wand and turned them into a heap of rubble.

All round the wreckage were pieces of fine glass. The pendulum must have flown out of Grandfather's insides as he crashed down because the springy piece of metal, stuck on to the shiny round thing that ticked steadily to and fro, was all twisted and bent. Both the weights lay on the carpet and all round them were tiny pieces of wood, pieces smaller than matchsticks.

Only when Sally's eyes had taken all this in did she pluck up the courage to pull the face of the clock out of the wreckage so that she could look at Grandfather's face. And when she looked she turned away almost at once. What had happened to it was too awful to see.

The fingers of the clock, once so beautiful, were bent double like hairpins and one had snapped right in two. The moon face still looked out at her, in its kindly way, but the four little girls were all scratched and spoiled. Sharp pieces of glass and metal must have been hurled against them in the fall. They were almost unrecognisable now; in fact they were more or less blobs again.

Sally turned her back on it all and sat down on the carpet, staring dumbly at the front door. She sat and stared for a very long time. The awful thing was that it felt such an ordinary day. Out in the street she could hear a little child talking to its mother. Then someone rode past on a bicycle, ringing a bell, and the church clock down the road chimed five. At the same moment Mrs Spinks Next Door banged three times on the wall. This meant 'Tea Time, Sally Bell', – it was a signal. It meant 'Lock up carefully and come back'. And it meant *immediately*. Mrs Spinks was strict about meal times.

Slowly, Sally went over to the little side window where people on the front door step could see into the hall. She pulled the curtains across, making everything dark. Nobody could look into their house now, nobody could see the remains of Grandfather, scattered all over the carpet. She went outside, pulled the front door shut and pushed her way through the dusty privet hedge to Mrs Spinks's house.

Only when she looked down at her plate and saw that it was cheese on toast for tea, did Sally remember William, who liked cheese very much, at any meal.

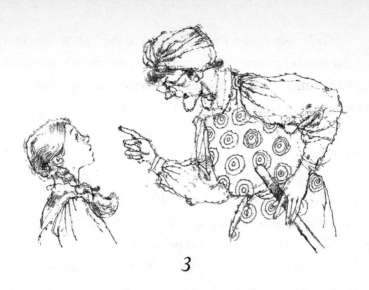

3

The day after the terrible thing happened was the day Amber had given Sally the phone number. It was also the day when Sally had to be very clever indeed. She had to make sure Mrs Spinks didn't go into their house *and see the clock*.

But what could Sally do? Mrs Spinks could let herself in at any time, she had the key. And she was the kind of lady who worried very much about burglars.

'I think I'd better pop in to your mum's, Sally,' she said at breakfast time. 'Just to check round.'

Sally must have gone very pale because Mrs Spinks said, peering at her, 'Bit off colour today are you, dear? Been to the toilet, have you?' (As well as worrying about burglars Mrs Spinks worried if you didn't go to the toilet regularly.)

Please, Sally said silently to herself, *don't let Mrs Spinks go next door*.

She really thought she was going to have to tell a lie. Perhaps she would tell Mrs Spinks that she'd dropped Mum's front door key down a drain. But then she had a brainwave.

She said, 'Mrs Spinks, I'm very sorry but my mouse has escaped from his cage. He'll be in our house somewhere but I really don't know where.' Then she added, 'He likes running up people's legs.'

This time it was Mrs Spinks who turned pale and she gave a little scream. 'Oh my goodness gracious. If I ever—' Then she turned her old-lady lips into the thin line. 'Sally Bell,' she said severely, 'until that mouse is back in its cage you must be a very grown-up girl. When you go to put his food out you must water your mother's plants for me. You must bring the letters over here and you must make sure there have been no—'

'Burglars. I know, Mrs Spinks,' Sally said in her most grown-up voice. 'And I'll look under all the beds.' Then she added, 'I might find my mouse.'

'*Ugh*,' said Mrs Spinks, fanning herself with the morning paper. 'I'm sorry, Sally, but if your mouse ran up my leg I think I should have a heart attack. When my Billie was a little boy we got him goldfish. There's never any trouble with goldfish.'

So at least Sally had arranged things so that Mrs

Spinks wouldn't go next door, and without telling a lie. But that didn't solve the problem of Grandfather. When people died you had to have funerals, she thought. So perhaps she could get a very big box, tip all the broken pieces in, and leave it out for the dustbin men.

But that didn't feel right. Grandfather Clock was like a person and you wouldn't leave a dead person out for the rubbish men. Also, there must be somebody in the world who could stick him together again. It now occurred to Sally that being able to get stuck together with glue was one way in which things were luckier than people.

It was because she was going to try with all her might to get Grandfather beautifully mended and ticking again, that she had needed Amber's special phone number, the one that got you through to God. Nobody else would do.

Sally woke up very early the day after Amber had given her the number, yawned, rubbed her eyes and got out of bed. It was the first day of the holidays and the sun was shining. No more school. Normally, she would have felt happy and light. Normally, she would feel like singing and skipping about. But today she felt as if there was a big stone on her chest, a stone that was crushing her. She felt all heavy. It was because of Grandfather.

She must go home straight away and phone that

number. She wouldn't have a wash till she'd done it, she would just put her blue dress on and slip out. With any luck, Mrs Spinks might not be up yet. She had a little lie-in on Saturdays, had a cup of tea in bed, and did the crossword puzzle.

But when Sally started to put her clothes on she found that her blue dress had turned into a red check one. Mrs Spinks had a craze about doing the washing. She must have decided it was dirty.

Sally crept out on to the landing and listened hard. Mrs Spinks's bedroom door was open and her bed was already made. She pulled on the red dress and went downstairs. But Mrs Spinks wasn't in her kitchen, she was in her wash house, a little brick hut across the back yard which you had to cross to reach the garden. Mum had a wash house, too.

The kitchen door was open. Sally crossed the yard and peeped round the corner of the wash house door. It felt all soapy and steamy and Mrs Spinks was turning the handle of a wooden mangle that squeezed water out of the clothes before they were hung on the line to dry. She was very red in the face. Mum had a mangle, too, but it was electric and went on its own.

Mrs Spinks liked turning the mangle herself. 'The old ways are the best,' she had told Sally.

'Hello, Sally Bell,' she said. 'You're up early.'

'So are you,' answered Sally. This must have sounded

a bit rude because Mrs Spinks gave her a funny look. But all Sally could think of was her blue dress. What had happened to it?

'Did you take my blue dress to wash, Mrs Spinks?' she said.

'I certainly did. It's soaking in that sink. I noticed you'd got all mud on it. Been down those allotments again, have you? Been sitting by that dirty old stream? My Jack used to come home filthy from those allotments. "Everything into the wash house, Jack". That's what I'd say to him.'

Sally said, 'I don't suppose you emptied the pockets, Mrs Spinks?'

Mrs Spinks blinked. 'No, I can't say I did.' Then she seemed to panic. 'You didn't leave anything like a pen in them, did you, because pens run something shocking and I don't want my washing all blue.'

'No, it wasn't a pen. It was… Oh, it doesn't matter. It wasn't important.' Sally didn't dare try and fish her dress out of the old brown sink. It would look too suspicious.

But it was quite easy to please Mrs Spinks. She beamed. 'That's all right then. Now, what about a bit of breakfast? Eggs on toast all right?'

Sally ate her soggy toast in misery. She liked scrambled eggs, but not when Mrs Spinks scrambled them because Mrs Spinks still used powdered eggs that you had to mix with water, the kind people had in the war, when you couldn't get fresh ones. It hadn't been the war for ages but Mrs Spinks said she'd got used to the taste.

It was watery eggs on soggy toast every Saturday morning. Lunch would be a plate of very sloppy stew with boiled potatoes, and tomorrow's lunch would be slices of dried-up chicken, and on Monday it would be fish cakes and mashed-up carrots. Pudding was always stewed fruit. The endless, pale-coloured meals stretched on and on.

Sally ate her breakfast very quickly, so that she could escape.

4

She would have to find Amber and get the telephone number again, unless, by trying really hard, she could actually remember it for herself. Appleford – it was definitely Appleford – 661, that was it! But then she wasn't sure. Could it have been Appleford 116? Sally thought and thought. She was certain it was one or the other. Then she had an idea. She could try both numbers; she could go home and use their own phone.

Mrs Spinks had a long thin garden with vegetables right at the end, and she'd gone out to see how everything was growing. Sally left a note on the kitchen table.

> Gone to feed my mouse and do plants
> Might go and see my friend Amber.
> Back soon.
> Love from Sally

Because she thought Mrs Spinks might be cross with her, for going off without permission, she added a few kisses, although Mrs Spinks was not really that sort of person.

'Appleford 661, Appleford 116, Appleford 661.' Sally kept repeating the numbers as she let herself into their house. She went quickly through the hall where Grandfather lay in pieces (she did not look at him) and along the corridor into the kitchen where the phone was. The plants were droopy and the kitchen had a stale, unused smell, but Sally went straight to the phone, before she forgot the numbers.

She picked up the telephone and a lady said, 'Number, please?'

'Appleford 116,' replied Sally.

'Hold the line, I will try it for you,' the lady said next and there were some clicking noises. But then she said, 'Madam, is it a company you are calling?'

Sally hesitated. 'Er, no, it's not a company. It's... I've been told I can talk to God, on this number.'

There was a little gap, then Sally heard the lady talking to someone, at her end, and laughing. Then she said, 'God what, Madam? What is the second name of the person you are calling, please?'

'There is no second name,' said Sally. 'It's just God. My friend told me the number was Appleford 116. But it could have been Appleford 661. I've got a bad memory.'

'Hold the line, please,' the lady requested. She had stopped laughing now and seemed more helpful. 'I will try that number for you.'

Sally waited. She heard three rings then the phone was picked up, and a man's voice said 'Hello? *Hello*?' He sounded very annoyed that Sally hadn't answered immediately. She said, 'I'm sorry to trouble you,' (that was how Mum always began), 'but I've been given this number for talking to God.'

'Don't be so damn silly,' said the man, and he slammed the phone down.

Tears stung behind Sally's eyelids. But then she thought of the heap of wood and glass lying all over the hall carpet, the heap that had once been Grandfather. Then she thought of Mum getting back from the hospital and walking into the hall, and seeing only a long shadow on the wall, where the clock had been, and she just knew she had to get it mended. So she picked up the phone again and asked the lady who answered (a different one this time) to try Appleford 116 again.

This time the lady managed to get a phone to ring, at her end of the line, so Appleford 116 *was* a real number! Sally held her breath. But the phone just rang and rang.

She was just about to give up when a voice said, 'Hello, this is the Paradise Centre. How may I help you?'

Her heart skipped a beat; this sounded more promising. Wasn't 'Paradise' something to do with God?

'How may I help you?' the voice said again.

'Um, I'm not quite sure,' said Sally uncertainly.

Quite suddenly the voice became very crisp and bossy. 'Well,' it said, 'we have several services we can offer you at this time. We represent Paradise Sales and also Paradise Holidays. And we have a new line, Paradise Pets. While you are away we can look after your cat and your dog. We can feed your tropical fish. We can—'

'Oh, I'm sorry,' Sally said, interrupting. 'I think I must have been given the wrong number.'

And before she could say anything else the crisp, bossy person had slammed her phone down. But Sally did not burst into tears, or crash around the kitchen in a rage, though she very much wanted to do both. She just sat on the floor and had a very long think.

At last, she stood up. She had made a decision. There was only one thing left to do. She must find Amber and get the correct number from her.

Very quietly, because Mrs Spinks might hear from over the wall, Sally went down the garden and pulled her bicycle out of the shed. She pushed open the back gate, closed it very quietly and pedalled quickly down the lane. This was the weekend the Fair left town and they would be packing up. She must hurry.

But when she reached the field where the Fair had been she found nothing left except a lot of paper blowing about. There were only some smoking black rings where fires had been and a little white dog that whined underneath a broken down cart, a dog that looked as if it had been left behind.

Quickly, Sally climbed back on to her bicycle and set off across the next two fields, towards the big main road and the lay-by where Amber's caravan had been. But she got there just in time to see the last of the caravans setting off, for the next town. Amber's was right at the back, pulled by a brown and white horse. It was buttercup yellow with a bright red chimney and it had been her great grandfather's. It must be as old as Mum's clock.

Sally started to pedal very fast, and to wave, and to ring her bell. 'Amber!' she shouted. '*Amber!*'

A face appeared in the doorway of the caravan. 'What do you want?' it said crossly. 'We're off to the next town.'

'Please stop,' Sally called out. 'I've lost that number. Mrs Spinks washed my dress and it was in the pocket. *Please*, Amber.'

'Please what?' The horse was clop-clopping quite fast along the road and Amber's face was turning into an egg-shaped blur, she was nearly out of sight. But Sally couldn't pedal any faster. She was puffing hard, and her legs ached horribly.

'The *number*!' she yelled. 'What was that special phone number?'

By now the yellow caravan was almost out of sight. Amber shrugged at first, and shook her head, but then, all of a sudden, she started to draw in the air with her finger. '6-1-6' she was writing then she yelled, '616! It's Appleford 616!'

At that same moment the caravans all disappeared round a bend in a cloud of dust, and Sally was all alone again, sitting in the grass at the side of the road and trying to get her breath back.

But her heart felt lighter. Amber had told her what she needed to know and what she had forgotten. How silly she had been, not to try the numbers in *that* order. It seemed so obvious now. Good old Amber. She could be so peculiar and grumpy sometimes but there was nobody quite like her. Sally climbed on to her bicycle again and pedalled back across the fields, and all the way home she repeated over and over again, 'Appleford 616.'

5

When she got back she saw Mrs Spinks outside the front door, bending over Mum's tubs with a watering can. 'Is that mouse back in its cage, Sally?' she said, as she came up the path. 'I think I'd better come in and check round. I did look through the hall window, but I see you've shut the curtains. Why?'

'Well, because of burglars, Mrs Spinks,' said Sally.

Mrs Spinks narrowed her eyes suspiciously. 'Mmm...' she muttered. 'If you promise to keep that mouse out of my way, I'll come in with you.'

Sally thought very rapidly. 'He's still out, Mrs Spinks, and – I know it's awful – but I've a feeling there might be other mice in our house, the brown kind. Mum finds droppings. She was thinking of getting a cat.'

Mrs Spinks shivered and picked up her watering can.

'I'll get back to doing the dinner,' she said. 'If you ask me, your mother should get the rat man in. Don't be long now, and mind you shut all the bedroom doors.'

'Yes, Mrs Spinks.' Sally wheeled her bicycle round to the shed, then came back to the front of the house and let herself in.

She walked straight past Grandfather, not stopping to look for signs of William. Instead she went down the hall that led to the kitchen, picked up the telephone and asked the lady to try Appleford 616.

After quite a few rings, someone answered. It wasn't the Paradise person and it wasn't the rude man who'd said 'damn'. It was a very old and creaky voice, a voice full of puffings and wheezings and it said, 'Appleford 616. To whom am I speaking?'

Sally's heart thumped. Then she plucked up her courage and said, 'This is Sally Bell here, I live at The Cedars, Villa Road, Broadfield. I am the daughter of Professor Thomas Bell and Mrs Ruth Bell. My father's Abroad and my brother's doing his National Service and Mum's in hospital and I have a really terrible problem—'

'I see.' There was a pause, then the creaking voice said, ' In what way can I help you, Sally Bell?'

Though it was the voice of a lady, and Sally had always imagined that God was a man, she felt encouraged because it sounded quite kind. So after a minute she said, 'Well, I was given your number by my friend Amber. She said that if you rang this number you could speak to God. She hadn't tried it herself because she said it was only for emergencies. Well, this *is* an emergency.'

The creaky old-lady voice said nothing to any of this. There were just a lot of wheezings. Sally waited, then she said, 'Hello, are you still there?'

'Yes, I'm still here, Sally Bell. Could you repeat what your friend told you, please? I'm a little hard of hearing.'

'She said that if you rang Appleford 616 you could speak to God.'

'I see.' There was another long pause, and more wheezings.

'So is God there?' Sally said. 'I really would like to speak to him.' Then she added, 'Please.'

'The person you refer to,' said the voice, 'does indeed live here. But he is in hospital, I'm afraid, like your mother.'

Now it was Sally's turn to pause. How could someone like God be in hospital, or even have illnesses? There must be some mistake. 'So I can't speak to him?' she said.

'I'm afraid not.'

Sally took the telephone away from her mouth and sat holding it, on the kitchen top. She didn't know what to do. All she could think of were the tiny little pieces of wood and glass that had been Grandfather, and of her mother opening the front door, and seeing them. The person who was called God was not available to help her. Sally began to cry.

She cried for a quite a long time. This crying kept on happening and she knew that it was because she was worrying more and more about Mum. Sally wasn't a cryer, not like some people. She was certain the lady would have replaced her telephone by now, which would be just as well, because she could be no help. But when she reached up to put the phone back, too, she could just hear the creaky voice saying anxiously, 'Little girl, little girl, please don't cry.'

'I'm not crying,' Sally said, then she added, 'now,' for she was always truthful (the bit about the mouse droppings was true, though it had happened a long time ago, and only once or twice).

'Would you be able to come to see me?' the lady continued. 'The person you wanted is too ill to be contacted at present but I just might be able to help.'

'Is it near?' Sally said. She had promised Mum she would stay with Mrs Spinks and not go anywhere big without her permission.

'From the end of Villa Road you could get the number Nineteen bus. Stay on for three stops and when you see the Appleford sign get off. My house is by the bus stop. It has a blue door.'

Sally looked at the kitchen clock. Mrs Spinks served dinner at one o'clock *on the dot*. But if the bus came quickly she might get there and back and not be late.

But ought she to go at all? She had been told never *ever* to talk to strange people and this was worse than talking to them. This was going to their house, on a bus.

She had decided she must say no when the creaky voice said, 'Is your father an archaeologist, Sally? Does he dig up strange and wonderful things?'

'Yes,' Sally said. He was quite famous but to Sally and Alan he was just Dad.

'He was once a little boy at my school. He was very good at sums and very bad at singing.'

'He can't sing in tune,' Sally said. Then she added loyally, 'But you can't be good at everything.'

'It would be best if you came now, Sally,' said the lady. 'I like to have my lunch on time, at one. Then I like to have a little rest.'

'I'll come at once,' Sally said. What the voice had said about lunch on time was the only bit which reminded her at all of Mrs Spinks.

6

The bus came almost at once and going three stops didn't take long. Very soon Sally was standing outside the blue door. Walking from the front gate to the house was like pushing your way through a jungle. Big trees hung over the pebbled path, and bushes and shrubs and creeping green things were growing all over the place. It looked as if nobody had done any gardening for years and years. The front door itself had ivy trying to grow up the corners but the creaky voice had definitely said 'blue door' and 'the house by the bus stop'. So Sally looked for a bell.

She found a big brass handle, a bit like the wooden

one that worked Mrs Spinks's downstairs lavatory. Under the handle was a card with curvy writing. It said *Mr G. Button* and *Miss A. Button*. Sally pulled it and from somewhere inside she heard a far-away tinkling noise, then the slow shuffling of feet.

The door opened and the voice she had heard on the telephone said, 'Sally Bell?' and she was looking down into the face of the smallest lady she had ever seen. 'Are you Sally Bell?' she repeated.

But Sally forgot to reply. She was too busy thinking, *Well, she's not all that small. Amber's granny's very little and Mrs Spinks is quite little, too.*

Then the little lady said again, 'Well, *are* you Sally Bell?'

'Oh yes, yes, that's me,' she spluttered, all in a rush. 'I mean, yes, that's who I am.' 'That's me' didn't feel quite correct, and the very little old lady sounded just a bit school teachery.

'Come in, then,' said Miss A. Button. She led Sally down a long cold passageway into a kind of greenhouse in which the walls and roof were covered with trailing plants whose leaves and stems had got all tangled together making a lovely greeny light. They sat down, in two creaking chairs made out of stuff that looked like raffia matting.

It suddenly went very quiet. The raffia chairs creaked and Miss Button made little wheezing noises in her chest, and some goldfish in an old sink kept plopping up to the surface with open mouths. 'They want me to feed them,' said Miss Button and she sprinkled some fish food into the water.

'Mrs Spinks says goldfish are a good idea,' said Sally. 'She says they're much better than mice.'

'Who is Mrs Spinks?'

'She lives next door. I'm staying with her while Mum's in the hospital. Alan's in the army now and Dad's Abroad. He's doing a very important Dig. I think it's in the desert. Mum says he mustn't be worried because she's going to get better very soon. But I don't think so. She's in a special room, in case she gets germs.'

'Which hospital, Sally?' Miss Button had leaned forwards in her creaky chair.

'The big white one, the one on the hill.'

'Oaklands Hospital?'

'I think that's it. But I can't go and see her at the moment, because of the germs.'

'I am very sorry, Sally,' said Miss Button. 'You do seem to have a lot of troubles.'

Sally didn't answer at first. Then, because Miss Button had a kind voice, and had been Dad's teacher when he was a little boy, she said, 'I've not told you my biggest trouble. It's why I phoned up,' and she explained all about the clock.

The little old lady listened very carefully. Then she gave the greedy goldfish a bit more food. Then she took off her spectacles, rubbed at them and put them on again. Then she looked at Sally. 'And that's why you wanted to talk to God?' she said.

'Yes,' said Sally, 'but you said he'd gone to hospital. I didn't understand that.'

'No,' Miss Button answered. Then she said, 'Sally, you seem like an intelligent girl. Did you really believe that, by ringing a telephone number, you could talk to God?'

'Well, Amber said you could,' Sally told her, 'and Amber's right about lots of things. She's not much good at lessons but she knows about all sorts of, you know, *special* things. I just thought this God person would be the one to talk to. I get these hunches.'

Miss Button thought for a moment, then she said, 'Sally, my brother is called Godfrey Button, and he is in hospital. He fell down the stairs and broke his hip. I think he is the person you were trying to speak to. I can't imagine how your friend Amber would know that some of his old friends used to call him "God", which was rather naughty of them I think. It was because his name is Godfrey, and also because he used to be in charge of a church.'

'Amber knows all kinds of things,' Sally whispered. Secretly she was thinking, *No God to talk to, only an old man whose friends joked about his name.* Just for a minute she felt as if the bottom had quite dropped out of everything. How could this help with the clock?

She said, 'Why was it naughty, calling your brother God?' She thought it was quite funny herself but she didn't dare say so.

'I suppose some people might think it wasn't very reverent,' Miss Button replied. 'I mean, you have to treat God with respect.'

'Have you ever seen Him?' asked Sally.

'Not exactly.' Miss Button looked down at the greedy goldfish and said quite snappily, 'You've had more than enough.'

Somewhere in the house a clock chimed once. That meant it was half-past twelve. Sally stood up. 'I'll have to go home,' she said. 'Mrs Spinks gets cross if I'm late for my meals.' Then she had a thought. 'Was that a grandfather clock striking? It sounded a bit like ours.'

'Well, sort of. It's a grand*mother* clock. It's a wee bit smaller than yours, I should think. Come along. You must go home in a taxi cab. I'll ring Ron.'

They went back into the chilly hall where a telephone stood on a table. Miss Button picked it up and asked for Appleford 123. *That was an easy number to remember*, Sally thought wistfully, thinking too of how she'd pedalled off so furiously, to find Amber.

'Arabella Button speaking,' said the old lady. 'Please

will you send a taxi to Seventeen, Norland Avenue. I have a visitor who has to get to The Cedars, Villa Road. It's Professor Bell's house. Thank you.'

'I think I would like to speak to your Mrs Spinks, Sally,' she said, as they waited. 'I think I should phone her. I would like to write to your father. I could send him a telegram, that would be quicker.'

But Sally clutched so hard at her thin old-lady arm that Miss Button jumped. 'Oh no, *please* don't talk to Mrs Spinks. You see, she doesn't know about the clock, or anything. If you could just... don't you know *anyone* who could help me? You've got a clock, too.'

Someone rang the doorbell and a voice said, 'Taxi to Villa Road.'

Miss Button opened the door and said, 'Good afternoon, Ron. This is Miss Sally Bell. She must be home by one.'

'Rightio,' the taxi man said cheerfully.

'But I have no money,' Sally whispered.

Miss Button put some coins into her hand. 'If there is any change you can give it back when we next meet. Could you be by your phone tomorrow at ten o'clock?'

'Yes,' Sally said, 'and thank you very much.'

It was steamed fish for dinner. The peas were a sickly bright green and the boiled potatoes had no taste at all. Sally said, 'Please could I have some butter, Mrs Spinks?'

Mrs Spinks pushed a pot of margarine towards her. 'Marge' was another war thing. 'This is just as good as butter,' she said. 'And it's cheaper. We all have to count the pennies, these days.'

Sally didn't want to annoy Mrs Spinks so she took a little piece of the greasy-looking marge and smeared it over her potatoes. But she was thinking, *I bet Miss Button has butter on hers*. And for the rest of the day she practised saying, 'I bet the Buttons eat best butter,' to take her mind off things.

7

Next day, Sally got up early. She mustn't be late for Miss Button, who seemed to be the sort of person who liked to be on time for everything.

She made her bed and tidied her room and brought her clothes down to be washed. Mrs Spinks seemed to wash every day. Mum wasn't like that. Their washing sat around for ages till it turned into a mountain; then Mum had what she called a 'blitz' and did it all in one go.

'I found this in the pocket of that blue dress,' said Mrs Spinks, as Sally came into the kitchen for breakfast, and she gave her a scrap of brown paper. 'Was that what you were looking for?'

Sally tried to look very casual. 'I suppose it must have been,' she replied, 'but it doesn't matter any more,' and she threw it into the waste bin. She'd got the phone number firmly fixed in her head now.

She was just getting the key from under the plant pot, to go next door to her own house, when Mrs Spinks called out from her pantry, 'Could you climb up and get some jam jars for me, Sally? I don't trust my old legs on this step ladder.' It was strawberry time and it looked as if Mrs Spinks had decided to make some jam.

Sally got the jars but they were all covered with dust and fluff. Mrs Spinks looked at them in dismay. Then she said, 'Now here's a nice little job for you. Fill the washing-up basin with nice soapy water for me, will you, and wash those jars.'

Sally glanced up at the kitchen clock, but Mrs Spinks noticed. 'Too busy this morning are you, Sally Bell?' she said, in a hurt kind of voice. 'Well, I'm quite busy myself. I'm going out soon but I've got to do my jobs first.'

'No,' said Sally. 'I'm not too busy. It's just that, well, I suppose I ought to go and try to catch my mouse. I'm late leaving his food out, and he'll be hungry.'

Mrs Spinks folded her arms. 'All right, off you go. Not sure we oughtn't to set a trap for that mouse of yours.'

Sally was horrified. 'Mrs Spinks, he's my *pet*.'

'I know, but mice are vermin, Sally. They carry diseases.'

'I think it's rats which do that, Mrs Spinks.' Sally's dad had told her all about the Great Plague of London and how rats had spread it. Then she added, 'Anyway, William is a very clean mouse. He's always washing himself.'

'Ugh,' said Mrs Spinks. It was the only word she had for mice.

As Sally let herself into the hall the phone was ringing. Sally ran down the hall, tripping over a fat blue letter that lay on the mat, grabbed the receiver and said, 'Hello, hello?'

'Did you oversleep, Sally?' It was Miss Button and she sounded a bit school-teachery again.

'Oh no. I was up early. But just as I was coming to phone you, Mrs Spinks asked me to wash some jam jars. I'm sorry.' The kitchen clock told her that it was just five minutes past ten. Old people seemed to be so strict about being on time. Would *she* be strict, when she got old? Sally wondered.

'Well, never mind. I have something to tell you.'

'Is it good news?' Sally said. 'Have you found someone to stick Grandfather together?'

'Not exactly,' replied Miss Button, 'but I have had some thoughts. Could you come with me to see my brother today, in the hospital? You could visit your poor mother at the same time.'

'I'm not allowed to see Mum yet,' Sally told her.

'Mrs Spinks rings the nurses each morning and they always say "not quite yet" and "wait a few days", things like that.'

'I see. Well, I expect they'll let you wave at her won't they?'

'I suppose they might...' Sally said slowly. But then she saw that there could be a serious problem. 'Miss Button,' she said, 'if I do come to the hospital it'll have to be a secret, because of Mrs Spinks. She mustn't know about the clock, you see.'

'Very well, Sally. I'm good at secrets. I'll send the taxi to collect you at ten minutes to two, shall I, then we can—'

'Oh *no*,' Sally interrupted anxiously (Miss Button couldn't be all that good at secrets), 'Mrs Spinks might see. I'll come to your house on the bus. There's some money left from yesterday.'

'Very well. Ten minutes to two it is, at my house,' said Miss Button and she rang off.

Before going back to Next Door Sally sat in the hall for a bit, with her back to Grandfather, and looked at the post. As well as the fat blue letter which was from Abroad, from Dad and addressed to Mum, there was a postcard for her. This was from Dad, too. The picture was a carved bird, black and beautifully polished, and the card said that the bird was four thousand years old.

There was a second card for Sally, from Mum in the

hospital, but it wasn't her writing. It said:

> A nice nurse called Rosie is writing this for me.
> Don't worry, our Sal. I'll be better very soon.
> Love and hugs,
>> Mum.
> P.S. Keep your eye on Grandfather for me.

(How Sally wished Rosie had not written that bit.)

Sally stared at the carpet. She felt funny. She felt all lifeless and tasteless. She felt like one of Mrs Spinks's dinners. And she was just sitting there, thinking of nothing at all, when William crept on to her hand with tiny pink feet.

She was very glad to see him. He was a warm, soft scrap of life in the dead house where no distant radio twittered, no piano played, no tall clock ticked. But she wished he hadn't come back because now she would have to capture him, and that would be the end of Mrs Spinks's staying away from their house.

She had already scattered his food just outside his cage. When he had finished washing himself he climbed down from her hand, scampered up to the cage door and began to eat. When every scrap had gone, he went inside and burrowed in his straw for a bit. But then he came out again and ran around the hall.

It was then that Sally got her good idea. Mrs Spinks

must be kept out of the house at all costs, and so long as she thought a mouse was running about she would stay away. Well, William didn't need to be shut in his cage. He obviously knew where to find his food. She wouldn't shut him in and she would be able to tell Mrs Spinks that he was still free. That way, he could have a little holiday while the clock was being mended, and Sally wouldn't be telling any lies.

So she gave him a bit more food, stroked his ears, then left him playing on his wheel inside the cage. Picking up the postcards and the fat blue letter, she went back to Next Door. Her next problem was getting away in enough time to be at Miss Button's house at ten to two. What on earth could she tell Mrs Spinks?

But she was in luck. When she got in Mrs Spinks was all in a flurry. There was a plate of fish-paste sandwiches marked 'Sally' on the kitchen table and next to it a small, old-looking apple and a glass of milk. Mrs Spinks was up in her bedroom and she was obviously getting ready for something. The house smelt of ironing and steam, and even perfume. The jam-making must be for another day.

Sally looked down at her sandwiches. Her word for fish paste was the same as Mrs Spinks's for mice. It was *Ugh*. But hearing footsteps on the stairs she took a little bite and tried to look enthusiastic. 'Going somewhere nice, Mrs Spinks?' she said.

Mrs Spinks was wearing a sky-blue raincoat, a sky-blue hat and carried gloves.

'It's the Bright Hour Ladies' Outing today,' she said. 'We are going to the sea. First we shop, then we have lunch, then we walk upon the sands. We go in a charabanc.'

'You have a lovely day for it,' Sally said politely (but what on earth was a 'charabanc'?). 'Thank you for my lunch.'

'I'm very partial to fish paste,' said Mrs Spinks. 'Your sandwiches all right, are they?'

'Mmm...' said Sally.

When Mrs Spinks had gone Sally wrapped the sandwiches in some newspaper and hid them at the bottom of the waste bin. What could the Bright Hour be? When she looked out of the front window she saw that it seemed to be about a lot of ladies in raincoats getting on to a shiny red and white coach that had stopped at the end of the road.

She had plenty of time to get ready for Miss Button's. The number Nineteen bus dropped her off at the house with the blue door at twenty minutes to two. She decided that being early was as bad as being late. Miss Button might be sleeping, or brushing her hair, or attending to the goldfish. So she waited patiently by the ivy-covered door until her watch said ten minutes to two o'clock exactly. Then she pulled the old-fashioned handle.

8

Miss Button must have been waiting behind the door because she came straight out, already wearing her coat and hat. It was a coat of many colours, patches of pink and purple and blue, and the hat had a peacock feather. Her shoes had quite high heels and they were purple, too. She was much smarter than Mrs Spinks in her blue raincoat.

'You look very nice, Miss Button,' Sally said.

'Thank you, Sally. I do think people in hospital should have jolly things to look at, don't you? And so should school children. I always wore jolly things in my classroom.' She looked at Sally. 'You look jolly too, dear.' Sally was wearing her favourite blouse, the one covered with little yellow roses which Mum had made for her. She was wearing the yellow skirt that matched. She had put her best things on, just in case they let her wave.

At the end of the jungly drive the same taxi man as yesterday was waiting. 'Oaklands Hospital please, Ron,' said Miss Button.

'Rightio,' Ron answered. 'Hop in,' and they were soon chugging up a long tree-lined hill. Right on the top stood a hospital, all white and gleaming, with a turret and some pointy windows. It looked a bit like a castle out of a fairy tale, and a bit like a factory...

Sally hadn't been there for over a week, not since they had put Mum in the special room. She hoped Miss Button's brother was in a different part. If she met a nurse who recognised her from last time she might tell Mrs Spinks.

But there was nothing to worry about. Mum and Mr Button were on different floors. Nobody looked at Sally anyway, though they certainly looked at Miss Button, resplendent in her rainbow coat and peacock-feather hat.

When she saw Mr Button, Sally's first thought was that he looked very like how she'd imagined God. He was sitting in a chair, with a rug over his knees, but even sitting down you could tell that he was extremely tall. He had a long straight nose and a wide mouth with curly edges and very large brown eyes. He didn't have much hair, just white froth stuck round the bottom of his skull, like a cake frill. But what really made him look like God was his beard. This was white and thick and very, very long – so long he could have kept his hands warm underneath it. Sally remembered that old people felt the cold badly and Mr Button looked very old indeed.

They sat facing him in two hard seats in which you had to sit straight up, otherwise you might fall off.

'How are you today, Godfrey?' said Miss Button.

The old man said, 'I'm doing nicely, Bella. They say I'm making progress. I should be home fairly soon. Did you bring the chocolate creams?' Though one was very tall and the other very short, both the brother and the sister had exactly the same old, creaky voice.

Miss Button took a box out of her bag and gave it to him. 'There you are. Not too many now. Bad for your teeth.'

The old man threw back his head and laughed. 'She's such a joker, our Bella,' he said to Sally. 'I don't have a tooth in my head.' He opened his mouth wide. There was nothing to be seen but a lot of shiny gums.

'I suppose that's one good thing about getting old,'

said Sally. 'I mean, you don't have to go to the dentist's.'

He looked at her. 'Yes, that's very true. Now, have I met you before?'

'I don't think so. But I did try to phone you.'

'Did you now? And why was that?'

Sally could feel her cheeks going red. 'I've got a terrible problem, and my friend Amber said that if I rang Appleford 616 I could talk to God.'

Mr Godfrey Button looked at his sister, then at Sally again, then he said, 'Now then, how would your friend Amber know about me?'

'I'm not sure. I don't know where she got the number from. But Amber knows lots of special things, she's that sort of person. Only—' Then Sally paused. The old man was staring at her so hard that his eyes had gone quite bulgy and sticky-out. He had a kind face. Even so, she felt a tiny bit frightened of him.

'Only what, Sally Bell?'

'You know my name,' she said, astonished.

'Yes, I know your name. Only what?'

'Well, I shouldn't have phoned, it was silly. But I do need to find someone to help me, someone who will know what to do, about my problem.'

'Someone like God?'

'I suppose so. Have you ever seen Him?'

'Not exactly,' the old man replied. It was just what Miss Button had said.

'Do have a chocolate, Sally,' he said, unwrapping them with his long clever-looking fingers. 'Isn't it wonderful to be able to buy all the sweets you want?' Because of the war you'd only been allowed to buy a few sweets each, but that was over now, though Mrs Spinks still bought war food.

'I know about your troubles,' the old man told Sally. 'Bella has told me all about them, and I've been having a very big think.'

'Have you reached any... conclusions?' asked Sally.

'Mmm...' said Mr Button. 'I've got a lemon cream. What have you got?'

'Strawberry cream,' mumbled Sally, with her mouth full. 'Well, have you?' she repeated, when she had swallowed the delicious chocolate.

'We think Mrs Spinks should send a telegram to your father and that he should come and see your mother, and look after you.'

'I meant about the *clock*,' Sally said firmly. 'Mum gave instructions. She doesn't want them to tell Dad, in case he comes rushing home when she's getting better all the time. I don't think it's easy to phone my dad, anyway. I think it's in the desert, where he's digging things up.' But both the Buttons had looked so very serious for a minute that Sally panicked. Perhaps her mother wasn't getting better at all. Perhaps everyone was just fobbing her off.

'I think the man you need to speak to about the accident is Charlie Bates,' said Mr Button.

'Does he know about clocks?'

'Oh, Charlie Bates knows about lots of things. He's a bit like your friend Amber.'

A nurse came in with a tray of cups. 'Tea time, Mr Button,' she said. Then she saw Sally. 'Hello,' she said, 'what are you doing here? You're on the wrong floor.'

'I came with Miss Button,' said Sally. 'Can I see Mum?'

'You can wave to her through the door,' the nurse said, 'but I'm afraid she can't have any visitors yet. Is Mrs Spinks with you?' she went on, looking round.

'No. Not today. She's gone off on a trip in a charabanc.' Then Sally said slowly, 'Nurse, please don't tell Mrs Spinks I came here today. I've come to... well, it's a secret, why I've come.'

'I won't tell. I'm good at secrets,' the nurse replied with a grin. 'I'm going down to Floor Two now. Why don't you come with me?'

Sally hesitated. ' What about Charlie Bates?' she said to Miss Button.

'Now off you go, Sally,' the old lady said firmly. 'I need to have a little talk to Godfrey about things. I'll meet you downstairs in the entrance hall.'

So Sally rode down in a lift with the nurse whose name was Rosie. She was the one who had written the postcard for Sally's mum. They got out at Floor Two and went down a lot of very shiny corridors and through several swinging doors. But instead of turning right, to the main ward which had lots of people in it, the nurse turned left, along another corridor.

At the very end was a room all on its own, and it had two lots of doors to itself. 'We have to be very careful about germs, Sally,' said the nurse. 'But look, there's your mum.' Then—'Oh dear, she's fast asleep.'

Sally peeped through the glass panel in the outer door. Mum was tucked up in bed very neatly, with her hands very carefully arranged on the covers. She looked so neat Sally could only tell it was Mum because of her mop of dark curly hair. Her face seemed very small and very white against the red hospital blankets.

'Best not to wake her,' whispered Rosie.

'All right,' Sally said. But even though her mother was fast asleep, she still waved, and she was still glad she'd put on her best things.

9

Miss Button arranged to telephone Sally in her house again, at ten o'clock the next morning. She said that by then she might have something to tell her about Charlie Bates. But although Sally sat by the kitchen phone for ages and ages, it didn't ring once.

When the clock said half-past ten, she picked it up and asked the lady for Appleford 616. After three rings a voice said, 'Yes?' but it wasn't Miss Button. This voice was chirpy and young.

'Is Miss Button there, please?' asked Sally.

''Fraid not. She's up at the hospital. It's her brother. By the way, this is Flo you're speaking to. I'm the helper.'

'What is the matter with her brother?' said Sally. 'I went to visit him yesterday. He seemed all right then.'

'Ah well, he had a little turn in the night. Couldn't get his breath, like. It might be a touch of yoomonia. Lots of old people get it.'

'Oh dear,' said Sally. After this bit of news she couldn't really ask about Charlie Bates, it would have seemed too selfish.

But Flo said brightly, 'You Miss Sally Bell, by any chance?'

'Yes,' replied Sally.

'Thought so. Got a pencil handy? There's a message here from Miss Button. Ready?'

'Ready.'

'It says, Charlie Bates, Two, Spodden Cottages, Appleford.'

Sally wrote this down very carefully, thinking that 'Spodden Cottages' sounded rather horrid. 'Is there a phone number?' she said.

'No, sorry. It says, Regret, does not have a telephone.'

'Um, Flo?'

'That's me.'

'You don't happen to know where Spodden Cottages is, do you?'

'Er-um, er-um,' said Flo. 'Is it... are they... they're by the canal, I think. Dirty old places. I thought they'd bin pulled down years ago.'

'Thank you very much, Flo,' said Sally and she put the phone down. She would go and see Charlie Bates at once.

But she had no idea where Spodden Cottages could be. The canal was a long windy one, they could be anywhere. Were they in Appleford or were they in Broadfield, the town where Villa Road was?

'Do you know where Spodden Cottages are?' she asked Mrs Spinks when she got back Next Door. The old lady was now very busy with her strawberry jam.

'Can't say I do. Unless... aren't they up Appleford way? Aren't they where the old gasworks used to be, near that smelly canal?'

'Don't know. I just wondered.'

'Why? Why did you wonder?' Mrs Spinks said sharply.

Sally thought fast. 'Oh, I just heard someone say "Spodden Cottages" and I thought to myself, Spodden's a funny name. Don't you think it is?'

Mrs Spinks looked at her as if she had just dropped in from another planet. 'I don't think about things like that,' she said rather disapprovingly. 'I have to get on with my jobs. Could you print me some nice neat labels, for this jam?'

'All right,' Sally answered. She didn't want to print labels one bit but it was important to get Mrs Spinks into a good mood so that she didn't start asking too many questions.

There was no way she could make the expedition to Spodden Cottages until two whole days later, when Mrs Spinks went to her Bright Hour meeting, at the chapel down the road. The Bright Hour Ladies sang hymns and someone gave a talk, and then they had cups of tea.

'Now I won't be back until five o'clock, Sally,' said Mrs Spinks. 'Perhaps tonight you will be able to visit your mum. That would be nice, wouldn't it?'

'Yes it would,' said Sally but in an unconvinced sort of voice. She knew that she wouldn't see her mother that day, and probably not for ages. They'd told Mrs Spinks it might take about six weeks. She still had this hunch that Mum wouldn't really get better till Grandfather started ticking again. She was certain that Miss Button would understand about hunches. But she hadn't telephoned Sally and this must mean that her brother still had the 'yoomonia'.

'There's trouble wherever you look, Sally Bell,' observed Mrs Spinks. All she seemed to mean was that the rain was pouring down and she was going to get very wet walking to the Bright Hour meeting.

If she only knew about my trouble, thought Sally, *she wouldn't worry about a bit of rain*.

As soon as Mrs Spinks had gone off to her Bright

Hour meeting, Sally fetched her bicycle from her garden shed and set off in the opposite direction, for Spodden Cottages. Although it was strawberry time and mid summer, it was a truly horrible day. The rain was coming down in great buckets and there was a howling wind. Sally's windcheater was sticking to her back as she pedalled along, and her thin summer skirt clung to her legs. It was raining so thickly she could hardly see.

But at last she found herself going down a bumpy lane that led to the canal, and in the distance she could see a big fat tower that looked like a gigantic cotton reel. This must belong to the old gasworks. Sally felt quite excited. She was getting warmer, closer to Charlie Bates's cottage.

But when she reached the tower she felt like going home. The gasworks were surrounded by a high wall of red brick and there were notices stuck all over it. They said 'Keep Out – Private Property' and 'Beware of Dogs'. She got off her bicycle to consult her map and leaned it against the wall, but it fell over with a loud rattling sound. Inside the wall a dog started to bark. Then a huge dark head appeared behind the bars of a gate and growled at her ferociously, showing great big teeth.

Sally snatched up her bicycle and made off very quickly, pushing it through sticky mud along the narrow tow path that bordered the canal. On the far bank was the long wall of a factory and the air had a nasty smell about it, the smell of something which had gone very, very bad.

The oily water was full of tin cans and rotting wood; she even saw a mattress floating along. Then a duck came by, followed by a troop of fluffy babies. Sally counted fourteen ducklings all striped like humbugs.

After the ducklings, the walk became very boring and just a bit creepy. On one side was the thick, dark canal water and on the other an endless tangle of trees and bushes. Their leaves were all dusty and stiff-looking, as if they hadn't done any actual growing for a very long time. And although she was a brave person, Sally felt a bit frightened. Someone could easily jump out at her from those bushes. If they did she would have to run for it, and leave her bicycle behind in the sticky mud. Would she ever dare to confess to Mum and Dad that she had been along this awful path?

But at last, when she had walked so hard she felt her legs were dropping off, it began to widen out. The dusty trees were replaced by a green field, in one corner of which there was a donkey munching at some long grass. Behind the donkey, Sally could see cars going past on an ordinary road and now there was a long tumble-down fence and a vegetable patch with wigwams of green beans, all bright with their scarlet flowers.

Then she saw a row of old cottages, not separate ones, but all stuck together. She got off her bicycle, leaned it against the fence, and looked at them. Which one was Charlie Bates's? To her dismay she saw that every single window seemed to be boarded up, and so were all the doors. Nobody lived here. She must have come to the wrong place.

She pulled out of her pocket the little map she'd made, of 'How to find Charlie Bates's house', and put her finger on the cross that said 'gasworks', then ran it along the canal path till it reached some black oblongs. 'Spodden Cottages' she had written on these. 'But it isn't,' she said out loud. 'It *can't* be.'

'Can't be what?' said someone. Sally looked up from her map. The voice had come from the middle of the vegetable patch.

'It can't be Spodden Cottages because that's where he lives and nobody lives here.'

'Oh, but they do,' said the voice and the bright red bean flowers began to rustle slightly.

Sally felt nervous. It was peculiar talking to someone you couldn't see. 'Er, could you come out?' she said. 'I think I've lost my way.'

She waited. 'Just a tick,' said the voice. Then, from the wigwams, a face emerged, then a whole body, and she was looking at a little fat man with a cherry red face and a spotted handkerchief knotted round his neck.

'I'm looking for Mr Charlie Bates,' Sally said.

'Speaking,' said the little man.

'Oh,' whispered Sally, 'it's *you*. But nobody lives here, it's all boarded up.'

'Is it really? That's funny. It must have happened while I was picking these beans. They're called Red Whoppers. They always produce a wonderful crop. Like beans, do you?'

'I'm not sure,' Sally said cautiously. Then she thought this sounded silly. People ought to know if they liked beans or not. So she added, 'Well, I like them when they're not cooked to a mush. That's what Mrs Spinks does, with everything.'

'Ah, Mrs Spinks. She's the old lady next door to you, isn't she? She's the one who doesn't like mice. I agree with her there. They're little perishers, mice are.'

Sally stared at the small red-faced man. 'How do you know about Mrs Spinks?'

'Oh, I know lots of things. For example, you're Miss Sally Bell.' He tucked the long green beans under one arm (they really were huge) and said, 'I think we ought to get down to business, and go inside before it starts raining again. Come along, Miss Bell.'

'But where to?' asked Sally, 'It's all boarded up.'

'Not quite,' said Charlie Bates. 'Everyone else has gone, but the wife and I are staying put. I was born here, at Number Six, and the wife was born next door.

Childhood sweethearts, you might say. If they pull down these old cottages, well, they'll have to carry us out of ours. They wouldn't do that, now would they, Miss Bell?'

'I hope not,' said Sally, and she followed Charlie Bates past the boarded-up cottages till they reached Number Six. It was the very end house and she could see now that it wasn't shut up. The windows sparkled and there was a neat garden with tubs of flowers by the door, and a black and white cat curled up on a windowsill.

The little man stopped at the front door and put his finger to his lips. 'I must ask you to speak very, very quietly, or not at all, if you please,' he said. 'The wife's laid up with a very bad leg and I think she's having a little nap.'

'All right,' Sally answered. Poor Mrs Bates. She must have fallen over. Mr Button had fallen down the stairs and broken his hip. Old people did seem to have lots of falls.

'Much obliged,' said Charlie Bates, and they went inside.

He made a sign that meant 'Would you like a cup of tea?' and Sally made a sign that said 'Yes, please,' and soon they were drinking it out of two beautiful blue cups with bird patterns on. There was also a sponge cake, light as air. Sally had eaten three pieces before she even realised. 'Oh dear,' she whispered. 'I'll get fat.'

Charlie Bates said, 'Have some more. The wife likes it to be eaten, that's what it's for.'

But Sally shook her head. 'I'm full up,' she whispered. Then she added, 'Did Miss Button tell you about me?'

'She did indeed. I know all about your troubles, Miss Bell.'

'But how?'

'A boy called Fred came, with a message. I think he works for Mr Moses, the butcher. He takes messages for people in his spare time, and runs errands, to make extra money. Now then, I gather that you tried to ring God.'

'Yes, I did,' whispered Sally. 'Are you one of the people that calls Mr Button God? Are you one of the old friends?'

Charlie Bates smiled. 'Yes, I would say I'm a very old friend.'

'Well, do you think it's all right, to call him God? Miss Button says we must show respect.'

Charlie Bates didn't answer but sipped his tea very thoughtfully. So Sally said, 'Have you ever seen God, I mean, the real one?'

'Not exactly,' said Charlie Bates slowly, which was just what the Buttons had said.

'Tell me about this clock of yours,' he went on. He

was speaking in a normal voice now, though very quietly. This must be because a gentle snoring noise was coming down through the beamed ceiling. His wife must be asleep just over their heads. 'I gather it took a bit of a tumble.'

'More than a bit,' said Sally.

'So what happened?'

'I was trying to wind it up. My mother's in the hospital, where God... where Mr Button is, and it had stopped. It stopped the very day Mum was taken into hospital, as if it *knew*. Anyway, my dad's Abroad, doing a Dig, and Alan's in the army, doing his National Service. So there was nobody left to wind it up but me.'

'And it fell over on you?'

'Oh no, I jumped clear. It was my mouse. He ran up the clock and frightened me and I grabbed at it and it came away from the wall.'

'All clocks should be firmly screwed to walls,' said Charlie Bates. 'It's not the first clock I've seen to that's fallen over.'

'But it *was* screwed,' Sally said rather fiercely. 'Dad did it. It must have worked loose. The point is, can you mend it?'

'I'm sure I can. There's nothing so bad that Charlie Bates can't put it right.'

'But it's in so many pieces,' Sally told him. 'There are hundreds of them.'

'Come with me,' Charlie said. 'I've got things to show you. No talking on the stairs now, we must let the wife get her beauty sleep. Got it?'

'Got it,' answered Sally, and she followed him out of the sitting room up a windy creaky staircase.

10

'This here,' said Charlie, opening a door at the very top of the stairs, 'is my clock room. Come and see.' Sally stepped inside and found herself looking down a long thin room with a pointy ceiling. All along one wall were windows with tiny square panes, and the floor was a pale gold colour and made of knotted wood. It was lovely and light and, outside, a big tree waved its branches, making the floor all dappled. Sally would have liked such a room as this to be her very own.

'This is where I mend things,' Charlie went on. 'Have a look round. Don't touch though. Some of the things being mended are at a very tricky stage.'

'I won't,' said Sally, setting off down the long, beautiful room.

It was full of clocks. Every kind of clock. Grandfather clocks and grandmother clocks and middle-sized in-between clocks. There were cuckoo clocks and there were wall clocks. There were mantelpiece clocks and there were carriage clocks. There were big ugly clocks with rusty hands, and there were little delicate clocks held up by beautiful china ladies. There was an alarm clock with two brass bells on top and there was a clock in the shape of Noddy. And though it was a mending room, quite a few of the clocks seemed to be ticking.

Sally glanced at her watch and saw that it was almost three o'clock. There was a whirring noise and the tallest of the three grandfathers began to strike, then a cuckoo clock said *cuck* and then the Noddy clock sang a little tune. The chiming and the bonging and the tinkling and the striking filled the air with a great jingle-jangle. Then there was silence again.

Charlie said, 'Anything here resemble your clock, Miss Bell?' putting his head on one side and looking like a very cheerful robin.

She looked carefully at the grandfathers and the grandmothers. They were all quite pretty but none of them was as pretty as the clock at home. These were much smaller and plainer. She didn't like to say so but not one of them was a patch on Grandfather; well, a patch on what he used to be.

'I'm afraid not,' she said. 'Our one is much bigger and fancier. I mean *was*. You can't call it a clock any more. It's just a lot of little bits.'

'Now that's not fighting talk,' said Charlie, taking her by the arm and leading her towards the twisty stairs. 'I've never been given anything I can't put right, given a little time. But the question is, how much time have we got?'

'Till Mum comes out of hospital.'

'And when is that going to be?'

'I don't know. At first they thought the illness would take about six weeks, I mean, to go away, but I don't think they know. They keep making excuses. The thing is, I'd like it to be done straight away, just in case.'

'I'd better come and see it then,' said Charlie Bates, when they had crept back down the stairs. 'And I shall have to bring it here, up to the mending room. If it's such a big feller, this clock of yours, I'll have to bring help with me, when I come to fetch it. I know, I'll bring Agnes.'

Sally didn't understand. If Mrs Bates was Agnes then she was laid up with a bad leg. How could she help? It must be some other lady, some rather strong person. 'All right, Mr Bates,' she said. She didn't like to ask too many questions.

'Would you feel able to call me Charlie?' the old man said in a shy voice. 'I know we are doing business,

77

over your clock, but it feels a bit more friendly, if you know what I mean.'

'Well, yes. Thank you very much... Charlie,' Sally replied. Her mum and dad always told her to use 'Mr' and 'Mrs' but it was different if someone *asked* you to use their first name.

'Good. And I'll call you Miss Sally. That all right?'

'Quite all right Mr... er... Charlie.'

He suddenly became very official and from a drawer took out a big blue notebook, a pencil and a pair of spectacles. First he wrote down Sally's address and telephone number. He wanted Mrs Spinks's number, too, but Sally said he couldn't really have that one. What if he got muddled, and got talking to her, and she found out all about the clock?

'Very well, Miss Sally,' he said. 'I don't usually telephone people anyway, not having one of my own. It's a long walk to the phone box from here. I'll send messages to Miss Button with the butcher's boy, shall I? And you can phone and get them from her. I won't need to get in touch with you too often anyway, with a bit of luck. We must get on with this job immediately. I'll collect Grandfather tomorrow from your house, and I'll bring Agnes.'

'Mrs Spinks mustn't see you.' Sally told him. 'She'll start asking you lots of questions, and she'll *find out*. It's got to be a secret.'

'Very well,' said Charlie. 'Give me a time when she is not on the premises and I'll come then.'

Sally thought for a moment. Mrs Spinks was nearly always on her premises. It would be another whole week before she went to her Bright Hour meeting and now she would be jam making again, or washing, or cleaning, or just plain snooping. It was very kind of her to look after Sally but for her part she couldn't truthfully say that she liked Mrs Spinks very much.

She thought for a little while and then she said, 'The only reliable thing about Mrs Spinks is that she always goes to bed early. She's sometimes asleep before I am.' (Sally knew this because Mrs Spinks was a very serious snorer.)

'Right then, I'll come after the lady's bedtime. What time is that?'

'She's usually in bed by nine,' said Sally. 'She has regular habits.'

'Very well. Agnes and I will be outside your house at nine-thirty tonight.'

'Could you come to our back gate?' asked Sally. 'The neighbours are a bit nosy round our way. They peep through curtains and things.'

'Rightio. Back gate it is,' said Charlie Bates and he wrote BACK GATE in his notebook, in big capital letters.

'Will it cost a lot of money?' Sally said.

'I need to see the clock first,' Charlie answered cautiously.

At that moment somebody knocked on the ceiling just over their heads. 'Charlie? Could you bring me my tablet, please? And a nice cup of tea? Ee, I'm that thirsty.'

'Coming, dearest,' he called back. 'Up in a jiffy,' and he led the way to the front door.

'Thank you for agreeing to do the clock, Mr — Charlie,' Sally said and she climbed on to her bicycle again, to ride back to Villa Road.

All the way home two strong feelings were having a fight inside her. One was hope. Charlie Bates was obviously very good at mending clocks and he was coming straight away to look at Grandfather. The other was worry. She knew it was going to cost money for all the things he would need. But he didn't look like a person with lots of money, and Sally herself had hardly any. She might have to tell him she could not afford his price.

Please, she said silently, *don't let there be a problem about paying Charlie.*

11

Waiting for Mrs Spinks to go to bed, the next night, was terrible. She kept fiddling with things in her kitchen while, on tenterhooks, Sally watched.

First she wiped the table over – when it didn't need wiping. Then she polished the kettle – when it didn't need polishing. Then she said she might stay up for a bit and watch the television.

Mrs Spinks was the only person Sally knew with a television set. Her grown-up son, Billie, who lived in Australia, had bought it for her, so she could watch the Queen's coronation. All the neighbours had squashed into her sitting room, to watch with her.

The set was very small with a bulgy-out screen and the black and white picture was always fuzzy, as if it was snowing. She was a little bit mean with her television set and she didn't switch it on very often, in case it wore out. She thought it should have little 'rests'.

When she said she was going to watch television Sally's heart came into her mouth. She might still be watching when Charlie came! 'Dad thinks television's bad for your eyes, Mrs Spinks,' she said. (This was true. He did.)

'*Really*?' answered the old lady, who wore very thick spectacles with lenses like pebbles. 'Well, I've great respect for your father... oh dear. Perhaps I'll have an early night instead. I might listen to my wireless, in bed. I need my sleep anyhow. I'm turning out the spare bedroom tomorrow.'

'Could I stay down here for a bit, Mrs Spinks?' said Sally. 'I'm not very sleepy yet.'

Mrs Spinks looked doubtful. 'Well it's your bedtime too, Sally Bell. Early to bed and early to rise, that's what I say.'

'But it is the holidays...' murmured Sally, trying to look pathetic.

'All right then, but only for a little bit. Now switch all the lights off, won't you, when you come up?'

'Yes, Mrs Spinks.'

Sally listened hard until she'd heard Mrs Spinks go into the bathroom, then come out again. Then she hung about in the kitchen for a few minutes, then she took up a position at the bottom of the stairs. The old lady always slept with her bedroom door slightly open. It was important to wait until the snoring began, before making a move.

It was twenty past nine before the first snores were heard. But Sally stayed where she was, waiting, until Mrs Spinks had got into a steady rhythm. It really was the most amazing noise to come from such a small lady. The louder snores sounded like the bellowing of a cow.

Just before half-past nine Sally stole through the front door. The street was empty and silent and there was no sign of Charlie and Agnes. She went back into the house, unbolted the kitchen door, crept down the garden and went into The Backs. This was the lane that ran along the back of the gardens, the lane where she had first learned to ride a bicycle and where little children played cricket. Some of the dustbins were painted with white stumps.

It was now exactly half-past nine and Sally was standing at the garden gate, staring up The Backs. At first she could hear nothing, then, quite far away, a little clopping sound began. It got louder and louder and quite soon something appeared at the end of the alleyway that joined up with Villa Road. Charlie Bates came into view, riding on a blue high-wheeled cart, pulled by a donkey.

Sally waved and Charlie waved back and almost at once he had stopped outside their gate. 'Whoa!' he said to the donkey which shook its ears, and made a loud *hurrumphing* noise. 'Shush, Agnes,' said Charlie, taking something from his pocket and feeding it to her. 'You'll wake Mrs Spinks.'

'Listen,' giggled Sally. Through Mrs Spinks's open window they could hear the awful snoring.

'My goodness me,' whispered Charlie. 'That's much worse than my missus, that sounds like a Force Ten Gale. Poor *Mr* Spinks.'

'I don't think there is one,' said Sally.

'I'm not surprised,' replied Charlie. 'I expect the poor man ran away, to try and get a good night's sleep. Now then, where's this old clock of yours?'

'*Follow me*,' Sally whispered.

Leaving Agnes and the cart in The Backs, she led him up the garden path and pushed open the kitchen door of The Cedars. 'I mustn't switch any lights on,' she said. 'People might see, and think it's a burglar.'

'OK,' said Charlie but almost at once he kicked a bucket over and sent it rolling across the kitchen floor with a loud clanging noise. The sound was huge and deafening in the still, sleeping house.

'Oh *heck*,' Sally whispered. 'I'd better find the torch. Stay where you are for a minute, Mr Bates.'

'Will do,' he said. She could hear him breathing in the darkness as she opened one drawer after another. Paper bags. Tea towels. A muddle of what felt like tin openers and wooden spoons. Mum was not a neat-and-tidy person like Mrs Spinks who had a little saying: 'A place for everything, and everything in its place'.

'Got it,' Sally said as her fingers closed on a heavy rubber torch. 'Hope the battery's still working. She clicked it on and a circle of yellow light lit up Charlie's cherry-red face.

'That's champion,' he said. 'We're in business.'

Sally led the way down the long passage to the hall. 'I'm not sure you will be able to do anything, Charlie,' she said. 'It's in so many tiny pieces.'

'Nonsense. It can't be as bad as all that. I've never yet seen a clock that—' But then, 'Oh dear, oh dear, oh my goodness me…' His voice had quite dried up. In the light of Sally's torch he could now see for himself what remained of Grandfather.

She felt a lump come into her throat as she watched his face. He scratched his head, and put it first on one side, and then on the other. Then he rubbed his nose. He was going to say it was hopeless, she knew he was.

At last he said, 'It's bad news, I'm afraid.'

'How bad?' whispered Sally.

'Well, I didn't expect it to be in quite so many pieces as this, Miss Sally. It must have fallen over with an almighty wallop.'

'But can't you do *anything?*'

'I don't know. I'm not sure I can take on a

complicated job like this, just at the moment, not with the wife poorly and everything. You see, Miss Sally, all my other customers are waiting for their clocks. And you say this is urgent.'

'Well it is, sort of. It's got to be done as soon as possible, in case Mum comes home.'

'Could you not speak to your daddy? He knows about old things, doesn't he? That's his job, isn't it?'

'No,' Sally told him firmly. 'I can't speak to him. He's Abroad, and he's not got to be told about Mum's illness. Not yet, anyhow. Those are her own instructions, to Mrs Spinks.'

'Well, you have a grown-up brother don't you? What about him? Can't he help?'

'No,' Sally said. 'He's in the army.'

Charlie Bates gave a big sigh, pulled hard at one of his ears and knelt down beside the broken clock. Then he began muttering to himself and for a long time all Sally could hear were things like, 'Snapped clean in two... both of them... That'll have to be riveted... Where does this bit go...' and a lot of little groaning noises that told her mending the clock was going to be quite impossible.

But when at last he stood up again he said, 'What we need, Miss Sally, are some cardboard boxes. Strong ones with lids. Got any shoe boxes?'

'I'm not sure. I'll go and look, shall I?'

'If you would. Meanwhile, I'll do some sorting.'

But Sally said, 'I'm afraid I'll need the torch, to go upstairs.'

Charlie Bates peered round the hall. 'Bring that little lamp over here,' he said. 'Nobody's going to see that from the road.'

So Sally brought the lamp and put it down beside him. Then she followed her wobbling torchlight up the stairs and into her parents' bedroom. Mum and Dad had a wardrobe each. Mum's was a muddle and her shoes were in a mad jumble at the bottom. But Dad was a very neat person. All his shoes lived in the boxes they had come home in.

She took three pairs out of three boxes and put each shoe very neatly back on the shelf, above Dad's rail of clothes. The lovely leather smell mixed with the smell of his old tweed jacket suddenly brought him very near. She needed him, she needed him very badly. He always knew what to do. What was *she* doing, creeping about their house with a torch while down below Charlie Bates sorted out bits of wood and pieces of glass? Why didn't she defy Mrs Spinks and *insist* that Dad was sent a telegram? He would come straight home then, and her troubles would be over.

But deep inside, Sally still had this secret hunch about the clock. She must put things right by herself. If she did, then Mum would get better. And anyway, it was that all her fault that Grandfather had fallen over in the first place. She should never have been so stupid as to think she could wind him up all on her own.

She came downstairs with the shoe boxes and gave them to Charlie Bates. 'Well now,' he said, 'how many pieces of wood do you think there are, in this pile?'

'I don't know,' said Sally, 'It looks like about a million, to me.'

'There are forty-three,' Charlie informed her, 'and most of them are no bigger than matchsticks. I've never taken on a job like this before, not in all my life.'

'I'm really sorry,' Sally replied, but inside she felt a tiny spurt of hope. It sounded as if he was at least going to have a go at sticking Grandfather together again. At least he hadn't said 'no'.

'Now, I'm putting the glass in this one,' he said, 'and the little pieces of wood in this one, and in this one I'll put all the bits of carving. But I suspect there may be more bits on this carpet. Here's a job for you, Miss Sally. I'm going to carry the big things out to the cart and while I'm doing that I want you to go over every *inch* of carpet with your torch, and see what you can find.'

'All right, Charlie.' And Sally got down on to her hands and knees straight away. While she was feeling about in the darkness William appeared. 'This is all your fault,' she told him. 'Mr Bates says all mice are little perishers.'

Charlie made three trips down the garden with the three big bits of Grandfather. Sally tried to carry one of the weights but found she couldn't even lift it off the floor. 'I never knew they were so heavy,' she said in astonishment.

'Oh golly, yes,' said Charlie. 'That's why your clock's in such a mess. Imagine one of these falling on you. *You'd* be in bits.'

Quite soon the three shoe boxes were arranged on the cart. Sally was pleased. She had found quite a few more bits, including one of the carved roses from the top of the clock. Charlie was pleased, too. 'The other one's all smashed up,' he said. 'I'll have to try and get a new one made. That's what costs the money, I'm afraid.'

Money. This was the part Sally could hardly think about. She had no money.

'I'll be on my way now,' Charlie Bates said, climbing up on his cart.

'So, what happens next?'

'Well, I'll need to look at all these bits, in my mending room and then—'

'Then what?'

'Then I'll send a message to the Buttons.'

'Will it be soon?'

'Couldn't say, Miss Sally, but I'll do my best. Can't do more than that now, can I?'

'No, I suppose not,' said Sally. She felt sad, now Charlie Bates was going home with all the bits of Grandfather. Agnes's neat little hooves had a sad kind of sound, too, as she clattered off into the darkness.

12

Next day, when Sally went to feed William and water the plants, she sat in the kitchen, by the telephone, and when the hands of the clock reached ten exactly she asked the lady for Appleford 616. After a lot of rings Miss Button answered.

'This is Sally Bell here,' Sally said nervously.

'Who... *who*?' said Miss Button.

Sally felt disconcerted. This was not at all promising. Could Miss Button really have forgotten her already? She waited for a minute then said, 'You know, I came to see you about the clock that had fallen over.'

There was a long pause at the other end of the phone and she could hear muttering. 'Clock... clock... what clock?' Then, 'Oh, of *course*, Professor Bell's little girl.

I'm sorry, my dear, but Godfrey had a very nasty turn, though he's rather better this morning. You must forgive me. Your trouble with the clock had gone quite out of my head. Now, what is happening, exactly?'

'Well, Mr Bates came and took it away, to mend.'

'Good. Very good.'

'Well, I'm not sure it is, I mean, yet. He told me that he could mend anything but when he actually saw it… There are forty-three pieces of wood, you see, and a lot more bits that I found on the carpet. Mending it might not be possible.' She nearly added that he needed some money, to buy all the things to mend it with, but she decided not to, in case Miss Button thought she was dropping a very rude hint.

Instead, she explained that, because Charlie had no phone and because they mustn't make Mrs Spinks suspicious, he was going to send Fred, the messenger boy, to the Button's house, and Sally would phone up for the latest news. 'Is that all right, Miss Button?' she asked.

'Perfectly all right, Sally. I know Fred. He brings me my Sunday joint, on his bicycle. Now, would you like to come to the hospital again, Sally? Your mother might be allowed to have visitors now.'

'I don't think she will be,' Sally replied. 'She's having tests. Mrs Spinks told me.'

There was a pause at Miss Button's end of the phone, then she said mysteriously, 'Ah, yes.' Then in a crisper sort of voice she added, 'Now, you will telephone me whenever you want to, won't you, dear?'

'Yes, Miss Button and… and I'm glad Mr Button's getting better.' But in her heart she was saying 'I wish Mum was, too'.

She decided to go back Next Door and count the money in her money box. There might be enough for a tube of glue. She could buy one and take it to Charlie at Spodden Cottages. But as she went towards the front door somebody knocked, and she could see the shape of a head, through the coloured glass. Sally opened the door, thinking it might be the postman, but it was Mrs Spinks. She charged in like a train, looking all pink and flustered.

'Whatever's the matter Mrs Spinks?' Sally said, backing into the hall and standing in the place where the clock had been, trying to look as tall as possible.

'Mrs Norris next door but one's been round to see me,' she said snappily. 'Told me she saw a light on here, last night. Now, you've not been leaving lights on, have you Sally Bell?'

'N… no, Mrs Spinks,' said Sally.

'So where's that mouse of yours, then?' said Mrs Spinks, suddenly looking down anxiously at her feet.

'He's in his cage. He's having a sleep.'

'Well, that's a bit of luck. Shut the door on him, if you please.'

Sally shut it, then went back to standing in the clock place. It could only be a matter of time before Mrs Spinks noticed that Grandfather had disappeared. But instead she set off up the stairs. 'Now, we must check all the bedrooms, Sally – under the beds, inside the wardrobes, everything. Come along.'

'All right, Mrs Spinks,' and Sally followed her up the staircase.

Mrs Spinks was very thorough and looked absolutely everywhere for signs of a burglar. There was no drawer she did not rummage in, no cupboard which she did not inspect. It seemed to Sally that she was rather enjoying looking at all Mum and Dad's things.

When she was quite satisfied nobody had been up in the bedrooms she started on the ground floor. This took even longer because there were a lot of rooms. 'You have such a lot of *stuff*, Sally Bell,' she muttered, flicking dust off a great carved eagle that stood on Dad's desk. 'And it's all so old, it's nothing but a dust-trap. I like new things myself. They're so much easier to keep clean.'

It was this liking for all things new that Sally thought might save her. Mrs Spinks still hadn't seemed to notice that the grandfather clock, the oldest and biggest piece of furniture in the entire house, was missing. But just as they'd reached the front door, to go home, she suddenly stopped in her tracks and turned back again.

'Something's different,' she said. 'Something's different, in the hall... now what can it be?'

Sally followed her inside again. 'I don't think so, Mrs Spinks,' she said, but with a sinking heart. Mrs Spinks wasn't listening. She stood in the middle of the hall carpet and sniffed the air, as if she could sniff in the answer, through her little snub nose. Then she exclaimed, 'I know! It's that great big clock. It stood there, didn't it, where that dark nasty mark is, on the wallpaper? Where's that gone then, Sally?' Then she looked very angry indeed. 'There *have* been burglars!'

'No. It went off to be mended, Mrs Spinks.'

'Mended? What for?'

'Well, it wasn't ticking any more. It needed, you know, seeing to.'

'Mmm... your mother fixed that up, did she?'

Sally was silent, then she said, 'Not exactly,' because it seemed a useful answer when you really couldn't tell the whole truth. It was what the Buttons and Charlie Bates had said, about seeing God. 'Not exactly', they'd told her, as if they'd seen some signs of Him, but not actually *Him*. 'It stopped when Mum got ill,' she added.

'Mmm,' Mrs Spinks repeated. 'I could have sworn... well, never mind. I must say there's a lot more room in this hall without it. As I said, I can't be doing with old things myself. Come along then. I must get the dinner on.'

Sally felt very relieved that Mrs Spinks had stopped

asking questions about the clock. She even tried to look enthusiastic about the dinner, which was a kind of grey mince with carrots mixed in. The taste was all right but it did look a tiny bit like sick.

Then Mrs Spinks made a really terrible announcement. She said, 'From now on, Sally, I am going to look after the key to your house myself. I feel uneasy in my mind. Mrs Norris swears she saw a light on last night. So if you want to go in for anything at all then you must ask me. Do you understand? We can't risk burglars.'

'Yes, Mrs Spinks,' said Sally miserably.

This meant that she couldn't go home to phone Miss Button to get Charlie's messages. It meant that she had to ask permission, not only to play with William but simply to *be*, in her own familiar place, with all its familiar things. All of a sudden she hated Mrs Spinks.

She ate most of the mince but when she had finished she left the table without eating her stewed apple. Instead, she crept up to her bedroom and had a private cry.

13

This time the cry didn't last long. Quite soon Sally had blown her nose, given her face a very good wash and felt much better. She had decided that she was not going to be beaten by Mrs Spinks.

She unlocked her money box with the little brass key and counted the contents. There were only a few coins inside because she'd been buying sweets. Until just a few weeks ago you had to have coupons to buy sweets — it was something to do with the war, even though it had been over for ages. But then they'd said people could buy as many as they liked again, and Sally had bought lots. Eating them took her mind off missing Mum and Dad and Alan, and off having to live with Mrs Spinks.

When she counted the money she realised that there wasn't even enough for a tube of fruit gums. This meant that there certainly wasn't enough for a tube of glue. Glue must cost quite a lot because Charlie Bates had said he'd need money, to buy all the things for the mending.

She went downstairs. Mrs Spinks was in her front room, talking to Mrs Norris about burglars. She never talked about nice things. If it rained she said, 'I could do with a bit of hot sun, to dry my washing', and if it was sunny she said, 'My poor tomato plants need a drop of rain'.

Sally crept through the kitchen and went up the garden to the vegetable patch. In one corner there was a little shed very like theirs. Sally went inside. She knew that this had been Mr Spinks's shed – Mr Spinks, who Charlie thought had left home because Mrs Spinks was a terrible snorer.

The shed was very neat and tidy with a lawnmower and a rusty old man's bicycle in one corner, spades, hoes and forks hung up on big hooks, and everything else on shelves. Sally ran her eyes along them. Everything seemed to be in tins and all of these were labelled. **Small Screws** she read, **Assorted Screws** then **Nails**… And *then* **Scotch Glue**, and next to this, **Best Glue**.

Sally did a little jump of excitement and reached up.

She was just tall enough to remove the two tins from the shelf. She shook them. They didn't rattle at all but they didn't feel empty either, in fact the **Best Glue** tin felt quite heavy.

She went back inside and climbed the stairs to her bedroom. She knew she had a problem. She would like to take the tins round straight away to Charlie Bates, but that would be stealing. And Sally had never stolen anything in her entire life.

She looked at the two tins. Both of them were extremely rusty. Nobody could want them now. They must have been in the Spinks's garden shed for years and years. She would just have to borrow them. If Charlie Bates used any of the glue then she would get Mum and Dad to give Mrs Spinks the money for it. She hoped this wasn't official 'stealing'. She couldn't think what else to do.

Then she had a thought. She took a piece of paper and wrote on it:

> Dear Mrs Spinks,
> IOU 2 tins of glue (1 Scotch Glue, 1 Best Glue),
> Yours truly,
> Sally Bell

And before going to fetch her own bicycle she put it on the shelf where the glue had been. She knew about

IOUs because Dad sometimes took the milk money to buy a newspaper and left one in the milk money tin for Mum. IOU was short for I OWE YOU, but quicker to write.

'Just going for a little bike ride, Mrs Spinks,' Sally called out as she went past the sitting room door. Mrs Spinks was talking to Mrs Norris about Mum being in hospital. She heard the words 'Doing more tests' and 'proper poorly' and 'poor little thing', which meant *her*.

'Well don't be too long, and keep off those busy roads.'

'Yes, Mrs Spinks.' Though Sally was thinking, *If she knew where I was going she'd confine me to the house. She'd probably tie me up.*

Now she knew the way to Spodden Cottages it felt very much nearer and because it wasn't raining and there was no mud she got along quite fast. The cotton reel gasworks tower came nearer and nearer and very soon she had reached the field where Agnes the donkey was, and the wigwams of beans. She leaned her bicycle against a hedge, took the tins of glue from the basket, and knocked on Charlie Bates's front door.

It was a long time before it opened and when it did it was only a crack. This was the way Mrs Spinks opened her front door, suspiciously. If it was someone she didn't know she always said, 'Not today thank you' and shut it.

Charlie poked his head out. 'Oh,' he said, 'it's Miss Sally.'

'Who is it, Charles?' said a voice from inside.

'Just a lady about a clock, dear, won't be a tick.'

Sally said, 'I found this glue, Mr Bates. I wondered if it was any use to you. I know that it's going to cost a lot of money, mending our clock.'

It was obvious that she was not going to be asked inside. Charlie was keeping her on the doorstep. He took the tins and tried to get the lids off, but they were stuck. 'Wait a tick,' he said, 'I'll get a screwdriver,' and he went inside.

Sally wondered why it had to be a secret. When he came out again she said, 'Doesn't your wife like it, when you mend clocks?'

Charlie turned pink. 'Oh she likes it, all right. Mending's what I do. But nowadays, we just have our old age pensions. It's quite hard to make ends meet. She says if I spend too much on bits and pieces for the mending, we won't be able to pay our proper bills. You see, Miss Sally, between you and me, some people never pay me at all for their clocks. They make promises, but they don't keep them.'

'I wouldn't do that, Charlie,' Sally said boldly. Then something made her add, 'Don't start on the clock till I've brought you some money.' She didn't know how she was going to keep this promise, she just knew she was going to.

'Now steady on, Miss Sally. Don't let's rush into things.' Very carefully Charlie levered the top off the Scotch Glue tin, then off the Best Glue one.

'Any good?' asked Sally.

'Mmm. It's very old. Look.' In the tins were what looked like a lot of tiny currants, all stuck together. 'You get boiling water and pour it on, and it melts.'

'It was Mr Spinks's. I just borrowed it. Shall I take it back?'

'No. I'll give it a go. It just might save us a few pennies.'

There didn't seem anything else to say, for the time being, and Charlie was clearly anxious to get back inside, to his wife.

'Haven't you finished yet?' she kept calling impatiently. 'I'll leave any message with the Buttons,' Charlie told Sally.

'I've got a problem now, about phoning,' Sally told him. 'Mrs Spinks has confiscated our door key. Someone saw the lamp, when you were looking at the clock. She thought it was burglars.'

'Oh dear, oh me,' said Charlie. 'Poor Mr Spinks. It wasn't just the snoring that drove him away, was it?'

As she cycled home Sally was thinking about the promise she had just made to Charlie. How could she get enough money together for him to start mending Grandfather? She would just have to earn it. But *how*?

Dad would know, she thought. Then she realised how silly that was. If Dad was here he'd know exactly what to do about getting Grandfather put right, and there would be no problem.

But Dad wasn't here, he was far, far away, Abroad. And Mum might as well be Abroad, too, shut up in that special room and nobody allowed to visit her.

14

Earning money to give to Charlie was very difficult. Sally thought she might as well begin with Mrs Spinks, so first thing after breakfast the next day she said, 'Are there any jobs I can do?'

'Jobs? What jobs?'

'Anything.'

'Well, that's kind of you, Sally. You could wash some more jam jars for me. I've got some lovely raspberries. I'm going to make another lot of jam.'

But there was no mention of being paid and Sally didn't know how to ask.

Mrs Spinks put three big boxes of jars on the table. They had come from her cellar and they were thick with dust and cobwebs. Sally saw a big spider scurry out of one, into a dark corner. It was only after washing and drying a whole box of jars that she plucked up the courage to say very politely, 'I was wondering if you could pay me a bit of money, for doing these, Mrs Spinks?'

There was a dreadful silence. Then Mrs Spinks said, in a hurt voice, '*Pay* you? Well I never. I thought you were helping me out of the kindness of your heart. Here, I'll do them myself.' She grabbed the tea towel from Sally's fingers and started to polish the jam jars vigorously. She looked extremely cross. 'After all I've done, and your poor mother stuck in that hospital…'

'I'm sorry, Mrs Spinks. I didn't mean to – it's just that I've got this project.'

Mrs Spinks sniffed suspiciously. 'Project, what kind of project? A school thing, is it?'

'Not exactly.' Then she felt bold. 'It's, sort of, about Mum.'

Mrs Spinks softened slightly. 'Oh, that's what it is. Well, why didn't you tell me? What are you doing? Saving up for a little present?'

'Sort of.'

It was true, in a way. If Charlie mended Grandfather, he might do it so nicely the clock would be even better than before the crash. That would be a present.

'Why don't you ask the neighbours if you can do jobs?'

'You mean, like Bob-a-Job? Like the boy scouts?'

'That's right. Don't go talking to strangers, though. Only ask the people in the street. Only ask the people your mummy knows.'

'That's a very good idea, Mrs Spinks.' Mum knew lots of people in the street, a lot more than Mrs Spinks, who was a bit of a gossip. If Mum's special friends hadn't all been away on their summer holidays any one of them would have looked after Sally. Mrs Spinks didn't believe in holidays, because of burglars.

When she had washed all the jam jars, and not been paid, she went out and walked down the street looking at people's houses. A lot of people had gone away, you could tell. There were rows of milk bottles on doorsteps, and uncut grass. But someone was in at Mrs Booth's house. Sally rang the bell.

'Hello, Mrs Booth,' she said, when the old lady came to the door. 'I've got to earn some money this week. It's for a project. Have you got any jobs I could do for you?'

Mrs Booth looked rather blank. 'Is it Sally Bell?' she said. 'How's your mummy, then? Is she home from the hospital yet? I heard she was proper poorly.'

'She caught something nasty, when she last went out to visit Dad. He's digging things up in a tropical country, he's Abroad.'

'Really?' said Mrs Booth. 'I don't believe in Abroad.

It doesn't do for people, you know. Well, give her my regards, Sally, when you go and visit,' and she started to shut the door. She had already forgotten why Sally had come.

'*Is* there any job I could do, Mrs Booth?' said Sally. 'I don't mind what it is.'

'Well now, I don't rightly know. I can't think of anything.' But then she said, 'When I was a little girl I used to go round collecting bottles. If you take some bottles to the shop they might give you some money.'

This sounded quite easy. 'What kind of bottles?' Sally asked.

'Wait there, dear, I'll show you one,' and the old lady shuffled back inside while Sally waited on the doorstep.

After about five minutes she came back holding two little brown bottles. 'This kind,' she said. The label said *Fanshawe's Fizzy Ginger*. 'It's wonderful stuff, this is,' Mrs Booth went on. 'It's very good for the bowels.'

She's just like Mrs Spinks, thought Sally. *She gets worried if people aren't always going to the lavatory.*

'You can have these,' the old lady said, 'to start you off. Good luck with your project. And give my regards to your poor mother.'

Sally took the bottles back to Mrs Spinks's and hid them in her bedroom. Then she found a carrier bag and set off down the street again. It was Tuesday and the next morning the dustbin men came. People had already put their rubbish outside their front gates.

Looking round first, just in case anyone was peeping, Sally started to rummage through the bags and boxes waiting on the pavement. The rubbish was dirty and smelly and covered with tea-leaves. No wonder the dustbin men wore thick gloves.

She found quite a few brown bottles belonging to Fanshawe's and she decided that a lot of the people in this street must have a craze for Fanshawe's drinks. That must be because they were mainly old, and worried a lot about going to the lavatory.

In the end her carrier bag was quite full. She took all the bottles up to Mrs Spinks's bathroom, locked herself in and washed them very carefully. Then she set off once again, this time to the newspaper shop in the next street. It was the kind of shop that sold everything and it was run by Mr Aladdin. Sally didn't know what his real name was but it said Aladdin's over the door.

'I've brought back these bottles, Mr Aladdin,' she said.

The shopkeeper was busy weighing out potatoes. 'Thank you very much,' he said. 'Put them there, will you? How's your mum, then?'

'Not very well. She's got a tropical disease. She's in a special room at the hospital.'

'Oh dear. Sorry to hear that.'

His customer paid for the potatoes and went out of the shop. Mr Aladdin rubbed his hands on a cloth and said, 'Now then, Sally, what can I get you today?'

'Well, I've brought these bottles back,' she repeated.

'Yes, I saw them. Thank you very much. Now what can I get you?' he repeated.

Sally didn't answer, she just waited. She didn't know what to say to Mr Aladdin, about the money. Talking about money seemed one of the most difficult things there was.

But at last she said, all in a burst before her courage slipped away, 'Don't people get money back on these bottles, Mr Aladdin?'

He peered at her over his little gold spectacles, then he rubbed his shiny chin. 'Come to think of it, Sally, I think they do. I'm very sorry. People don't return bottles to me very often. I'm out of the habit.'

'Well, please may I have the money due? It's for a project.'

Mr Aladdin started counting the bottles. 'There are fifteen,' Sally told him.

'Fifteen bottles, hanging on the wall,' said the shopkeeper, humming a little hum as he opened his till.

Sally felt rather excited, especially when she saw Mr Aladdin put some coins into a little paper bag, and twist it shut at the top, like sweets.

'There you are,' he said. 'Any time you have Fanshawe's bottles to return, I'm your man.'

'Thank you, Mr Aladdin,' said Sally, and she hurried back to Mrs Spinks's.

When she was up in her room, with the door shut, she counted out the money. There were thirty round brown pennies, two for each bottle.

Sally was so disappointed she felt a cry coming on, but she swallowed back the tears. It was no good crying all the time. Perhaps people didn't really give you money in return for bottles any more. Perhaps Mr Aladdin was just being kind. At least she knew that she wasn't going to waste any more time poking about in smelly dustbins.

She posted the pennies through the slit in the top of her pig and lay back on the bed. There had got to be a faster way of earning money.

15

Next day, Sally decided to visit Mr and Mrs Box at Number Seventeen. They looked quite rich. Their house stood all on its own in a large garden, and by their front steps was a shiny black car. Only three lots of people owned cars in Sally's street and the Boxes were one of them. Mum knew the Boxes because they did good deeds and sometimes came round collecting old clothes for people in need.

Mr and Mrs Box were tall and thin, like sticks, and they wore pale brown clothes. Their house was brown, too, and it had a funny smell, a bit like cabbage and a bit like hospitals. She didn't like that particular smell because it reminded her of Mum in the special room. When the Boxes saw her standing on their doorstep they pulled long, sad faces. 'We are so sorry Sally, about your mother,' they said in a chorus. 'Why don't you come inside for a few moments?'

So Sally went in. She really didn't want to explain about Mum being very ill any more and about why Dad hadn't been told. She had a secret feeling the Boxes knew anyway. They were the sort of people who always got to know things. So she went straight to the point. She said, 'I have to raise some money, for a surprise I'm preparing for my mother. It has to be ready when she comes home. Have you any jobs I could do?'

The Boxes looked at each other and their eyebrows started going up and down. They seemed to be saying things to each other without actually speaking. Then Mrs Box unfolded her long skinny legs from under her and said, 'Wait in here, Sally, we will need to consult.' And without a word, they both left the room and shut the door on her.

The consulting took ages but at last the Boxes opened the door again and summoned her into their garden. 'We have consulted,' said Mrs Box. 'Mr Box and I can offer you some weeding work. Our garden turned into a wilderness while we were away on holiday. Come and see.'

So Sally followed them outside and down the long

narrow garden. It didn't look at all like a wilderness; it looked very, very neat. The grass was cut short, within an inch of its life, the dark fir trees at each corner stood rigidly to attention and every flower grew exactly as it had been told.

'Where are the weeds?' asked Sally.

'Ah, you are very kind,' said Mr Box. It was the first time he had spoken and his voice was dry and papery thin. It seemed to be coming from a very faraway place. 'There are millions of weeds, though some are only just starting to grow. You have to get them young, Sally, like *this*.'

He bent down and tweaked something out of the bare brown soil with his long thin fingers. The green stalk was tiny but Mr Box addressed it in a ferocious voice.

'How will I know what a weed is?' Sally said. 'My mum has a saying that a weed is only a flower in the wrong place.'

Mr and Mrs Box exchanged bland, flat smiles. 'How quaint,' said Mrs Box. 'But of course, you have a very *different* garden from ours, don't you?'

'I suppose we do,' Sally said, thinking of their rambly, jungly garden with its ancient apple tree, its greeny pond where the frogs were and its clumps of nettles where Dad threw the grass mowings.

'Can you start straight away?' said Mrs Box. 'We

have some visitors coming on Saturday. We would like the garden to be weed-free by then.'

'Yes,' said Sally. 'I'm not doing anything else this afternoon.'

The Boxes gave her a carton to put the weeds in then marched off into their neat brown house. Sally made a start but it was extremely hot. The soil had been baked to a crust by the sun so pulling out the tiny weeds was not very easy. Often only bits of grass came up, and the root stayed behind. She was sure this wouldn't count as an official weed but she threw the grass in anyway.

All the time she was working she could see the Boxes sitting in two tall narrow chairs, watching her through a window. From time to time Mrs Box came out and inspected the weeds in the carton. 'Mm...' she said. 'You must be more brutal, Sally, you're not pulling up the tiny ones.'

Sally didn't feel like being 'brutal', she felt sorry for the little plants, already wilting in the cardboard box. Some were very pretty, with masses of starry white and yellow flowers.

It got hotter and hotter. The sweat poured down her cheeks and ran into the corners of her eyes. She would have liked a cold drink but the Boxes didn't bring her one. They just sat in their tall brown chairs and waved at her encouragingly through the window.

Sally thought wistfully about Amber. *She* wouldn't have agreed to do this weeding. She would have got the money for Charlie Bates in a more magic way, or she might have prayed to God. It was now so hot Sally decided she'd have to stop weeding before she fainted, but at that very moment the Boxes came out of their house.

'I have brought you a drink,' said Mrs Box. 'Fanshawe's fizzy lemonade. It's extremely good for you.'

'I know,' Sally replied, drinking gratefully. 'Er, perhaps I could take the bottle back to the shop for you?'

'That's very kind, Sally, but it's one of Mr Box's little jobs, to return the bottles. You get money back, you see.'

Sally didn't answer. She was beginning to suspect that Mr and Mrs Box were not very generous people, even though they collected old clothes for poor families. And she was right. Before they paid her for the weeding they counted the weeds in the box twice, because they disagreed over the number, and then they gave her ninety-four pennies. 'That is two pennies for every weed you've pulled, Sally.' Mrs Box handed over the money with a generous smile. 'Now when *I* was a little girl I only got *one* penny for pulling weeds.'

'Thank you very much,' Sally mumbled, putting the coins into her pocket. She thought Mrs Box must be at least sixty years old. One penny all those years ago must be worth a lot more than two pennies now. She felt cheated. Mr and Mrs Box were very, very mean.

'I have to go home now,' she said. She had pulled the last weed she was ever going to pull, at least from the Box's garden. She hoped all the tiny weeds she had not bothered to remove would grow big, and scatter their seeds, and grow into a jungle.

On her way home she went into a phone box and rang Appleford 616. Flo answered.

'This is Sally Bell speaking,' said Sally. 'I just wondered if there were any messages for me? And, how is Go— how is Mr Button?'

'Hang on,' said Flo. 'There's something written down here. Er-um, er-um… oh yes, Mr Bates "can't get on with the job." Er-um, er-um… "Needs a picture. Please draw clock. Or send photograph." That make sense does it, Sally?'

'Sort of,' Sally said slowly. 'And how is Mr Button?'

'Heaps better,' Flo answered cheerfully. 'The yoomonia's gone. He's doing well. Any message for Miss Button?'

'Just tell her I rang, please.'

'Will do.'

When she got back to Mrs Spinks's she counted her money. There was only one pound and twenty-seven pence so far, to give Charlie Bates.

She felt very depressed. It would take her weeks, if not months, to earn enough money for the clock. There had got to be other ways. But she couldn't think of any. She decided to try and draw the clock for Charlie, to take her mind off things.

She went down to the kitchen, where she could spread out. Mrs Spinks said, peering over her shoulder, 'Oo, that's nice. That for your mum, is it?'

'Sort of.'

It was funny but although Sally had known the grandfather clock all her life, she couldn't remember exactly what it looked like. For example: How many carved roses had decorated the top? And how many of those spiky things had there been? She made separate little drawings of everything, making up the bits she'd forgotten. Then she took a fresh sheet of paper and did drawings of the four little girls. She could remember these rather better. How would Charlie get them back to normal, though? They had been beautifully painted and now they were so scratched by the broken glass they had almost disappeared.

'Mrs Spinks,' she said, when she had finished. 'I'd like to go next door for a bit.' Charlie had asked for a photo of Grandfather and if she looked through all Mum's snapshot albums she might find one.

But to her surprise Mrs Spinks sat down beside her, and put a hand on her arm. This was unusual because

Mrs Spinks wasn't at all a kissy or a touchy person. She said in quite a gentle voice, 'Not just now, Sally, I have something to tell you.'

Sally shivered. Then she braced herself inside. 'Is it about Mum?' she whispered.

'Yes, I'm afraid it is. She's taken a bad turn, in her illness.'

Sally shot to her feet and said in a very fierce voice, 'Well I want to go and see her, Mrs Spinks, and I think you should send my father a telegram now, this minute.' Nothing was going to stop her going to see her mother. Even if she was unconscious they couldn't stop her going to see her, they just couldn't, could they?

But Mrs Spinks said, 'I'm afraid you can't go and see your mother at the moment, Sally. They have transferred her to a special hospital in London. Now you are *not* to worry. The doctor has told me that they know everything about tropical things, and about Abroad, in this new place. With luck your mummy will be right as rain in no time.'

'But… is my dad coming home?' Sally said.

'Not yet, but the hospital knows where he is and they *will* contact him, if they decide that is the best thing to do.'

'You mean if she gets worse, don't you?' said Sally suspiciously.

Mrs Spinks pretended not to have heard this. 'Now

you get on with your drawing, there's a good girl. How about if I make us a bit of tea? How about a few rock cakes?'

'No thank you, Mrs Spinks.'

Mrs Spinks's rock cakes were uneatable. In fact, they were exactly like rocks. 'I'd like to go for a little bike ride,' she added, 'to take my mind off things.'

'All right, dear.' And this time, perhaps because she knew she had just delivered some really awful news, Mrs Spinks did not remind Sally about watching out for cars on the road.

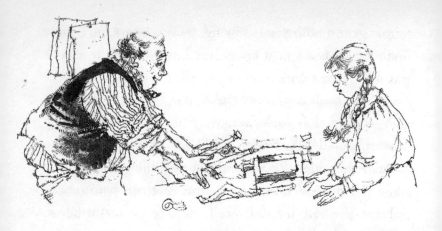

16

Sally went straight to Charlie's with her drawings. This time, when he opened his front door, he beamed and whispered, 'Come in, come in. The wife's having a nap. Mum's the word, of course,' and he put his finger to his lips.

Sally followed him through the sitting room, with its chunky oak beams, up the creaking staircase and into the clock room. It was exactly five o'clock and before they could speak to each other they had to wait for the bonging and the chiming and the tinkling and the cuckooing to die away.

Then Charlie took her by the hand and led her down the room till they reached a long table. This had a neat label stuck down flat, along the front edge. *Repair of Miss Sally's Long Case Clock*, it said, in neat black letters, and underneath was the date when Sally had first come to see him at Spodden Cottages. Next to this was a clipboard with a lot more dates. *Collected clock from The Cedars, Villa Road,* it said, then, *Started sorting the mahogany pieces (53 altogether)* then, *Sorted painted pieces (44 altogether).*

After each item, Charlie had written the time it had taken to do these things. It looked very, very official and there were lots of funny words as well like 'cramping' and 'riveting' and 'beading'.

Sally said, 'Have you done any actual sticking yet, Mr Bates?'

'Oh dear me, no. I've been sorting. I'm waiting for you, Miss Sally.'

'Well, I've made you some drawings,' she said, and she gave them to him.

Charlie looked at them carefully, turning them this way and that. 'Well I must say, you're a good little drawer. These will help me a lot. Er, this bit, Miss Sally, at the very top. What goes there? You've left a big gap. There should be a lovely piece of carving in that gap, It's what they call "the finishing touch". Now, do you have any photos of the clock?'

'I think we might have,' Sally told him, 'but I'll have to go home to look for them, and now Mrs Spinks holds on to the key it's much more difficult. She gets suspicious.'

'Anything else?' Charlie asked next, in an embarrassed kind of voice. 'I've got to buy some special clamps, you see, to hold the pieces together, while the glue dries. And a man I know is going to do a bit of new carving for me. And another man is going to re-paint the little girls. It all costs quite a few pennies I'm afraid, and that old glue is no good, I'm sorry to say.'

'Well, I've brought some pennies,' Sally told him and she tipped them out of the brown envelope she'd put them in, into his outstretched hand.

Charlie looked at the coins, then put them in tidy piles on his workbench. 'Hmm,' he said. 'Well, that'll buy me a few screws and things. Thank you, Sally.'

'But it's not enough, is it?' Sally asked him.

The old man shook his head. 'If I'm honest, not really, not if you want this job doing double quick, like you said.'

'I do,' Sally said firmly. 'My mum's got worse and my dad might have to come back from Abroad. I really, really do want the clock ticking again, Mr Bates. It'll make her better, I know it will.'

The old man looked at her. 'Will it, now?'

'Yes.'

Then Sally heard herself saying a most extraordinary thing. She didn't know where it had come from, the words just seemed to leap up from somewhere deep inside her, demanding to be spoken out loud. She said,

'When I next come to see you, Mr Bates, I'll bring enough money to get the clock mended at once, and more besides.'

'And more *besides…*' repeated Charlie. 'Well now, that really would be something. I'll look forward to that. Meanwhile, I'll keep sorting and counting shall I, into these splendid shoe boxes?'

'Yes please, Mr Bates,' Sally told him very firmly, and she cycled home.

That night, before she went to sleep, Sally sat on her bed and closed her eyes very tight. Then she cleared her throat. 'Hello, God,' she began, 'this is Sally Bell speaking. I'm not sure you're there (as far as she understood it God knew everything about you, so there was no point at all in pretending), but if you are, please listen to me.

'I'm very worried about two things. First, my mother is very ill. They've just taken her to London and put her in a hospital for tropical diseases. They still don't seem to know what's wrong with her but she must be quite bad because Mrs Spinks said they might send for my father and Mum had said they mustn't do that.

'The second thing is, as you know, my mouse ran up the clock and frightened me and it fell over and broke into lots of pieces, ninety-two, to be precise. Charlie

Bates says he can mend it but some other people have got to do the special things and he has to pay them. Please could you send some money so he can get on with it? He's an old-age pensioner and I don't think my weeding money, eckcetera, is enough. Also, his wife doesn't like him doing jobs without being paid. I don't blame her, though I must say she sounds a bit of a nagger.

'I don't mind doing lots of jobs myself, to earn the money, but please could you give me some quickly as I've got this hunch that Mum won't get better until Grandfather Clock is mended. I hope this doesn't sound silly. Yours sincerely, Sally Bell.'

After a little thought, she added her name, address and telephone number and then, 'P.S. It's an emergency, and Amber said that was what you were for.'

She got into bed thinking about what Miss Button had said, about treating God with respect and whether she had done, saying all this to Him, just as if He was an old friend. And while she was thinking about *this* she fell deep, deep asleep.

17

Next day Sally earned some clock money quite by accident. It was Tuesday, the day when Mrs Spinks did her Big Shop and went into town on the tram. Sally was in charge of the house. She had not been allowed to go next door. Mrs Spinks had done that herself, very early. She seemed very determined to keep Sally away from The Cedars.

Dad had sent her another postcard. She was just reading it and feeling very sad, when somebody gave a long, long ring on the doorbell. Sally opened it.

'Elsie?' said a voice (Elsie was Mrs Spinks's first

name) then, 'Oh, it's *you*, Sally love. Where's Elsie? I've got a problem.'

The person who had rung the bell came into the hall and flopped down on a chair. It was a lady called Linda Smellie, and she lived three doors down. Sally liked Linda a lot. She was a bit fat, and she had big flat feet that slapped along the pavement when she walked up the street and her hair, which was long, was always falling into her eyes and flying about.

It must have been awful, having the name 'Smellie', though Dad said it was a very old Scottish name and that you should pronounce it 'Smiley' and that, anyhow, you mustn't *laugh*. Sally didn't laugh. She felt sorry for Linda because she'd got two little children and her husband had run off with her very best friend and left her on her own, with no money.

'Mrs Spinks isn't here,' Sally told her. 'She's gone to town, to do her big shop. It's Tuesday.'

'Oh heck,' said Linda, then she grabbed Sally's arm. 'Well, listen, love, can you come and mind our Edward? I've got to take our Martin to the doctor's. I shouldn't be long, there's a taxi waiting.'

'What's wrong with him, Mrs Smellie?' Sally very much *didn't* want to mind Edward Smellie. He was the noisiest baby in Villa Road, and when he cried his great big mouth turned into a letter box slit. But she felt very sorry for Linda.

'Well, yesterday he rolled up a tram ticket and stuck it up his nose and now he's feeling proper poorly. I've rung the doctor and he said bring him straight down. Can you come, Sally love? I'll pay you, for babysitting. I know you're saving up for your mum and that.'

So Sally scribbled a little note to Mrs Spinks. *Gone to look after Edward Smellie at Number Eleven*, then she followed Linda up the street.

Five minutes later, she watched her get into a taxi with Martin, who was grizzling and whining. He was always doing silly things like sticking rolled-up tickets into his nose.

The minute she went into Linda's house, Edward started crying. It was as if stepping on the doormat had pressed a secret button, and started him off. She went upstairs, following the sound of the hoarse, shrieking voice. It was stuffy and dark in Edward's room and it smelt strongly of baby and dirty nappy. But she didn't dare try to change him, she might drop him on his head, or stick the pins in him. She made what she hoped were quiet, soothing noises and the crying instantly stopped. 'Good boy, Edward,' she called from the doorway, then she crept downstairs.

The living room wasn't very nice. It was a brown sort of room with a thin brown rumpled carpet and a huge plastic wireless, also brown. There was a saggy-looking settee along one wall and a table covered with dirty dishes. Sally decided to tidy up a bit, for when Linda came back.

She'd just filled the kitchen sink with some hot soapy water when Edward started crying again, then shrieking, then bawling. This time when Sally went up, he wouldn't stop, his voice just got louder and louder, and his fat little face was such a bright red he looked as if he might explode. There was nothing else for it, she would have to take him downstairs again.

'Look, nice wireless,' cooed Sally. 'Look, nice carpet. Look, nice newspaper,' pointing at everything. None of these things was a bit nice but they were all she could think of, and they kept Edward quiet.

When he'd not cried for about ten minutes she put him back in his cot and this time, to her great surprise, he fell asleep at once. She managed to finish the dishes, pick up the rubbish from the floor and even found a few flowers in the garden, to put in a vase, when he started crying *again*... And this time, he did not stop, whatever Sally tried to cheer him up. It was awful.

At last, completely exhausted, she sat down in an armchair, and held Edward very tight. Then she found herself humming a little tune, then singing some words.

Golden slumbers, kiss your eyes,
Smiles awake you, when you rise,

Sleep pretty darling, do not cry,
And I will sing a lullaby.'

The minute Sally started to sing the baby stopped crying and stared up at her. He had big dark eyes the colour of violets, and he seemed to be smiling. 'Did you like that, Edward?' whispered Sally.

'Uh-uh,' he grunted and she decided that meant 'Yes'.

So then she sang everything she knew: lullabies, nursery rhymes, jingles from the wireless adverts, and Edward was perfectly happy. But after a while she realised that she was falling asleep, instead of the baby, so she clutched him even tighter, and began to sing the only song she had not used up. This wasn't exactly a baby song but something with strange and beautiful words that she had once heard her mother sing.

'I met at night the Prince of Sleep,
He had a sweet and lovely face.'

And gradually, they *both* fell asleep.

A very long time afterwards Sally woke up with a start, still holding the baby who was now very damp but beautifully asleep. Linda was standing over her, and Martin was sitting on the soggy settee sucking an ice-cream lollipop.

'It's for his sore throat,' explained Linda. 'They got out the tram ticket with some tweezers. Would you like a lolly, Sally love? I've got plenty.'

Sally looked at Linda's kitchen clock. 'Er, I would. But can I eat it at Mrs Spink's? She'll be back from shopping, I should think, and I've been here ages.'

''Course, love. Have a couple.' Linda went to the fridge and came back with two lollipops. She wrapped them in a piece of newspaper and then started rummaging in her handbag. 'This is for you, love. I know you're saving up for your mum.' And she pressed something into Sally's hand.

She looked down and saw something crinkly and brown. It was a ten-shilling note. She was astonished and a little bit of her wanted to cry. Ten shillings was a lot of money. In fact, she'd only ever had one ten-shilling note in her life. 'Linda,' she said, 'you can't give me all this. I only looked after Edward.'

But Linda took Sally's fingers and closed them over the note, one by one. 'I can if I want. You've done me a good turn and you've done wonders with Edward. Anyhow, I want you to get something really great, for your mum and... and when she comes home, we'll give her a party, shall we?'

'Well, all right, Linda,' Sally said reluctantly. 'I *am* saving up for something.' She couldn't help thinking of the Boxes, and how generous they'd thought they'd been, about the weeding money, and about their comfortable house and shiny new car, and then about Linda's place.

Linda gave her a great big hug, and Sally hugged her back. It was the first proper hug she'd had for a very long time. She didn't much want to go back to Mrs Spinks's.

After dinner, Sally asked if she could go home for a bit. She said she wanted to look for some photographs.

'Not now, Sally,' said Mrs Spinks. 'I've got my pantry shelves to rearrange, after all the shopping. Can't it wait?'

Sally looked at the floor and pouted. Then she said, 'I really don't see why you won't let me, Mrs Spinks. The photos are for the project I'm doing, for Mum. Why can't I?'

Mrs Spinks turned her mouth into the thin straight-line shape it always assumed when she couldn't get her own way. 'I've told you, Sally, I'm uneasy in my mind, when you're there on your own.'

'I'll come back in half an hour, I promise. *Please*, Mrs Spinks.'

'Oh... very well, then.' And with a dramatic sigh Mrs Spinks handed over the key. Sally knew she had only said yes because Mum was so ill, and she went straight home in case Mrs Spinks changed her mind.

As soon as she got inside she phoned Appleford 616. Miss Button answered almost at once but she seemed to be in a great hurry. She was going to the hospital to see her brother Godfrey.

Sally said, 'Miss Button, please will you help me?'

'Of course,' the old lady replied. 'Is it about the clock? Are the repairs going well?'

'Charlie's still sorting all the pieces out,' Sally told her. 'I've made quite a bit of money from babysitting, and I did some weeding for Mr and Mrs Box, and I took some bottles back to Mr Aladdin.'

'I see. Good. That will certainly help things along. Every little helps. Was there anything else, Sally? I really must go. Ron has just rung the doorbell.'

Sally opened her mouth, then she shut it again. What she wanted to say was too big and too scary. The words wouldn't come out.

'Sally? Are you there?'

'Yes,' she answered in a miserable mouse-like whisper.

'Tell me, what is troubling you, dear?'

'My mum's been sent to a tropical hospital in London, Miss Button. I don't think they know what's wrong with her. *And Mrs Spinks won't send Dad a telegram*.' She said the last bit very forcefully.

There was a short silence on the other end of the phone, and a funny pondering sort of noise like 'Er-um, er-um', which was what Flo always said.

Then Miss Button said, 'What is the name of the new hospital, Sally?'

'I don't know. But they might know at the old hospital.'

'How sensible. I shall ask them. Now, Sally dear, I don't want you to worry. You get on with your clock project, and your little jobs. It will take your mind off things. I am sure the new hospital is going to sort your mummy's illness out very soon. Meanwhile, I shall think what is best to do. Now, are you all right, Sally?'

'Yes, Miss Button.'

'Good girl,' and she rang off.

Sally looked through Mum and Dad's photo albums until she found a picture of Grandfather. It showed her and Alan in his brand-new army uniform, standing on opposite sides of the clock. It was a very good picture and you could see everything quite clearly, even the four little girls that were the seasons of the year. She removed it from its page then put the albums back on the shelf. She didn't want to look at them any more than she had to. Seeing all the happy family pictures had made her feel sadder than ever. She very much hoped Miss Button would do something now, about telling Dad to come home.

It was time to go back to Mrs Spinks's. But as she went towards the front door somebody rang the bell.

She opened it and saw the delivery boy from Mr Moses the butcher, standing on the doorstep. He was holding a brown paper parcel. 'Special Delivery,' he said. 'Name's Fred. Am I speaking to Miss Sally Bell, by any chance?'

'Yes, that's me,' Sally replied.

'OK. Sign here, please, and print your name underneath.'

Sally took the pencil he held out to her and wrote her name twice. What could this be? Special Delivery things were usually for Dad. But it was her name on the label.

'Thanks very much, miss.' The young man handed over the parcel and walked down the path. Then he climbed on to a huge black bicycle with a big basket on the front. A little dog had got up on to its hind legs and was sniffing at something in the bottom.

'Hey!' shouted Fred. 'Those are Mrs Heggerty's sausages!' and he pedalled off smartly.

Sally stood on the doorstep having a more careful look at the neatly written label, just to make sure that the parcel really *was* for her, and not for Mum, Dad or Alan; then, with a fluttery kind of feeling starting up inside her, she made her way back to Mrs Spinks's house and went straight upstairs. She was going to open this parcel in strictest private.

18

Only when she was safely inside her room, with the door shut, did Sally open the parcel, which she now saw was more of a thick, squishy envelope. First she looked again at the writing on the label. It wasn't the writing of anyone she knew. And the sender hadn't put their own name on, in the corner. It felt very mysterious and that was why Sally had got this fluttery feeling.

When the envelope was undone, she put her hand in and felt round. Her fingers closed upon something soft and slightly moist. The feel reminded her of the time when she was very very little, when Dad had brought a baby hedgehog in from the garden, to show her and

Alan. Though it was terribly prickly it had a soft pink tummy, softer than velvet even. Whatever the soft thing was inside this parcel, it felt a bit like that pink little hedgehog tummy.

Very carefully, she took it out, and looked. It was a squashy bag, pulled tight at the top with a drawstring and it was made, not of skin, but of the softest yellow leather.

Sally looked at it, then gave it a shake. The bag chinked gently and now she could see little bulges all over it. It was too heavy to hold in one hand for very long so she got off her bed and sat on the floor with it. Clearing a space on the carpet she loosened the drawstring, which was also made of leather, and opened up the mouth of the bag. Then she turned it upside down and tipped the contents on to the floor.

Always, for all her life, Sally thought she would remember that moment in Mrs Spinks's spare bedroom because what she saw, tumbling out of the dark leather inside, were silver coins, hundreds of them, raining down in a glittering shower on to the swirly pink patterns of the carpet, chinking and winking and blinking in the sunshine that had suddenly started to pour through the window, making the room all gold.

She caught her breath, then closed her eyes very tight, almost certain that when she opened them again the heap of shiny silver pieces would have disappeared.

It was probably all a dream and she was going to wake up with a nasty jolt. But when she did open them the coins were still there, and the great burst of sunshine had become a steady glow, as if the sun himself had settled down to see what would happen next.

Sally picked up one of the coins and looked at it closely. It was a half-crown coin with the King's head on it (there weren't many with the Queen on yet). All the other coins looked exactly the same. They were not grubby, dirty coins, they were beautifully shiny, as if the person who had put them in the bag had polished each one very carefully, before popping them in. But who could have sent her this bag of money? She felt inside again, this time for a letter to explain where it had come from, but there wasn't one. Then she had still another look at the outside of the envelope, but there was no clue at all about who could have sent it.

Sally sat on her bed again and looked down at the silvery carpet under her feet. She knew that she must try very hard to solve this amazing mystery, but not yet. She had a very urgent errand to do and she must do it at once.

She picked up the silver coins in handfuls and put them back in the bag. Then she felt all over the carpet and under the furniture, in case some of the coins had rolled out of sight without her noticing, but none had. She pulled the drawstring very tight again and put the leather bag back into the squishy envelope, then she got out her school satchel and put the envelope inside that. She slung the satchel on to her back, and pulled the leather straps nice and tight. She was not going to be parted from this bag of silver for a single minute.

Please let Mrs Spinks say yes, she whispered to herself as she made her way down the stairs, but Mrs Spinks had gone out. A note on the kitchen table said:

> Gone round to Mrs Norris's for a cup of tea. Back soon. Be a good girl.

> Gone to see a friend. Back soon too.

Sally added underneath, and went straight to the shed to get her bicycle.

When she reached Spodden Cottages, Sally found Charlie Bates in his front garden weeding a flower bed. The sun had shone on her all the way and it was still shining. It was warm and all the cottage windows were open.

'Mr Bates,' she began, all in a rush. She was dying to tell him about the money. But he put his fingers to his lips and wagged his head at the open windows. Sally dropped her voice to a whisper. 'Mr Bates, I've got some brilliant news,' she said.

'Charlie? Who is it, dear?' Mrs Bates must have

heard, from up in her bedroom.

'Only Miss Bell, dear, about her grandfather clock. Won't be a tick, then I'll put the kettle on.'

By now Sally didn't need any special instructions about going up very quietly to the clock room. She knew now that Mrs Bates was a grumpy sort of person and didn't much like Charlie mending clocks. She also knew that the Bateses had five grown-up children and fourteen grandchildren and that they needed money for all sorts of things. Charlie had promised Mrs Bates not to spend their pension money on mending clocks for people that didn't pay. And Sally had said she wouldn't make him break that promise.

Now she didn't have to. There was plenty of money for Charlie. There was a whole bag of silver half crowns!

On his work bench, Charlie had set out Dad's three shoe boxes very neatly and there were some other boxes, too. Each had a label: *left hand side, right hand side, middle. Cramps, rivets, beading.* Sally was dying to ask what some of these mysterious-sounding words meant but she was dying even more to show Charlie what she had brought. 'Please could you clear a space?' she asked him.

Charlie cleared one. He and Sally understood each other now. He didn't have to ask what the space was for. Just the sound of her voice had told him it must be for something very important.

Sally said, 'Fred the delivery boy brought me a present and I know it's for the clock. I hope you will accept it, and start at once.' She put the shiny coins in a heap in the middle of the bench. When Charlie saw the thick silver pennies heaped up all shining his little round eyes grew as large as saucers. 'But I... Miss Sally... where has all this money come from? I've never seen so much money, well, not all at once.'

'I don't know,' Sally said. 'Perhaps it's a miracle.' She thought that miracles were supposed to be something to do with God and she'd just remembered that last night she'd tried talking to Him, before she went to sleep.

'Please will you count it?' she asked Charlie. 'I said that next time I came I'd bring the money for the clock. But will this be enough, do you think?'

'I'm sure it will, Miss Sally,' Charlie answered in such a peculiar voice that Sally wondered whether he was trying not to cry. As she very much didn't want him to she said very briskly, 'Should we put it into little piles?'

'Yes, let's,' replied Charlie. So they started counting.

'Well, eight half crowns make one pound,' said Sally, and she put eight in a neat pile. Then Charlie added another pile and so they went on and when all the shiny silver coins had been arranged in these neat piles and the neat piles arranged in neat rows, all along Charlie's workbench, they counted them, in a deep silence during which neither of them said a word.

'I reckon we've got about a hundred piles here,' said Charlie. 'We can't have, surely… *can* we?'

'I think you're right,' Sally answered, then she added, 'Wow!'

'But I think we'd better—'

'Count again? So do I.'

So they did, very carefully, but it still came to the same number. 'Plus ten shillings,' said Sally, remembering her babysitting money which she now folded up and put under one of the piles.

'So how much do you think we've got, Miss Sally?' whispered Charlie. They had both gone very, very quiet, as if they were in the presence of a great mystery. 'Here, let's both work it out,' he said, and he got them both some paper and two very sharp pencils. Sally had noticed that Charlie's pencils were always nice and sharp.

They both knew already how much money there was, but it felt so important that Sally pretended to do some sums and wrote down a number. Charlie wrote one down, too. Then they put their pieces of paper side-by-side on the workbench.

One hundred pounds Sally had written and Charlie had written £100.

'Plus Mrs Smellie's ten shillings. Linda hasn't got

very much money and I only minded Edward for a bit. But she said I must accept it and I didn't want to hurt her feelings.'

'Quite right,' said Charlie. So they both added another ten shillings to their pieces of paper. There was a little pause while they both looked at the piles of coins. 'Is a hundred pounds and ten shillings enough?' Sally said anxiously. She knew that it would take hours and hours to stick all the tiny pieces of Grandfather together again and that Charlie would have to buy a lot of special things, and pay people to do the painting and the carving, too.

'It's more than enough,' Charlie told her. 'You could buy a nice little car with a hundred pounds. I reckon it's more than enough, in fact it's exactly as you said.'

'What did I say?' Sally had quite forgotten.

'You said that next time you came to see me you would bring all the money we needed, and more besides. When the clock is ready I'm sure I'll be giving you a lot of this back again.'

'Keep it for now,' Sally told him. 'You never know.'

So Charlie took a new piece of paper and wrote *Receipt* at the top, in lovely curly writing. Then underneath he wrote:

Received from Miss Sally Bell, on account of clock repair, one hundred pounds and ten shillings.

He signed his name and gave her the paper. 'I shall write down exactly what I have to buy,' he said, 'and how long everything takes, and I'll give you back what I don't spend. How's that?'

'Wonderful,' replied Sally. But she was looking doubtfully at all the boxes of bits. 'Do you really think you'll be able to do it?' she said. 'I mean, so that nobody can tell?'

'I'll do my best,' said Charlie. 'But it's a bit like putting together the world's most difficult jigsaw when you don't have the box with the picture on, to help you. Know what I mean?'

Sally nodded her head. Dad loved doing hard jigsaws. She'd been so excited about the bag of silver that for a while she'd forgotten about Mum getting worse and having to go to the hospital in London. But she was thinking about it now and how much she wanted her father to come back from Abroad.

'I'd better go home now,' she said, 'or Mrs Spinks'll get cross.' But just then she remembered the photographs and she got them out of her satchel, and gave them to Charlie. 'Are these any help?' she said.

Charlie looked at the pictures carefully and made a little purring noise. 'Well now, Miss Sally,' he said, 'these are going to help a lot. And you were quite right, there *is* a gap at the top, isn't there, where the maker would have put his finishing touch? Look, there should be something between those two wooden roses.'

Sally looked where his finger was pointing. 'Yes,' she said, 'but isn't it funny? When I did the drawings I couldn't remember what the clock looked like, properly.' And she started to fasten the straps of her satchel again.

'Here, take the little bag with you,' said Charlie. 'It's beautiful soft leather.'

'I know,' replied Sally, taking it, and she gave it a sniff. As well as the lovely leather smell there was the faint smell of something else, something perfumy and a bit spicy. She had never smelled anything quite like it before.

Sally pedalled home very quickly, thinking about what might be happening to Mum and getting up all her courage to insist on going to their own house for a bit, on her own. It was wonderful about the bag of silver, but now she had given the money to Charlie she had gone back to thinking about her mother again. She wanted to phone Miss Button and tell her to send Dad a telegram straight away. She had a horrible feeling that Mum was now very ill indeed and that they weren't telling her, and this horrible feeling just wouldn't go away.

19

When Sally got back, Mrs Spinks was still out but she decided to ring Miss Button, from the phone box at the bottom of the road. Mrs Spinks said using the phone all the time cost too much money. Sally wanted to know if she had spoken to Dad yet, about Mum being taken to the special hospital, or to the doctors themselves.

She went straight upstairs, took some coins for the phone call out of her moneybox and came down again, and she was just walking to the front door, past Mrs Spinks's telephone, when it rang.

Sally picked it up. 'Hello,' she said, 'this is the Spinks's residence,' (which was exactly what Mrs Spinks had told her to say) when a voice at the other end said, 'Hello, is that my darling girl?' and it was Dad.

All of a sudden Sally's knees felt wobbly, so she sat down on the carpet, in case her legs should give way under her. But she still held on to the phone very tight. 'Dad,' she said. 'Where are you? Are you Abroad?'

'No, sweetheart, I'm in London. I'm with Mum, in the hospital. Your friend Miss Button sent me a telegram, then a doctor phoned me, so I came, just as soon as I could jump on an aeroplane.'

'Is Mum better?' asked Sally. 'Can I come and see her yet? How long have you been here? Why didn't you ring me *before*?'

Dad said, 'Slow down, Sally, slow down. Let me answer one question at a time. I've been ringing and ringing but you never answer. You're not at Mrs Spinks's and you're not at home.'

'That's because I'm not allowed to go home much. Mrs Spinks has taken the key away.' Then she added, 'Dad, it wasn't a good idea, Mum sending me to stay at Mrs Spinks's. She can be horrid.'

'Oh dear, that's not good news. Would you like to go and stay with Uncle Bill and Auntie Pauline?' said Dad. 'They're back from their holidays.'

'No,' replied Sally. 'I want to come to London. I want to be with you and Mum. I want to come *now*.

When can I?'

But Dad gave what sounded like a little sigh, and said nothing at all.

'Well, *can* I?' repeated Sally. 'Dad… *Dad*? What's the matter? Has Mum got worse?'

'Oh no,' Dad told her. 'It's a marvellous hospital. There are millions of nasty bugs around to make people ill, in the very hot countries, but they think they know what Mum's bug is now, and they're on to it.'

'What do you mean, "on to it"?' Sally said rather suspiciously.

'Well, they know what kind of medicine to give her now, to kill the bug. They didn't before.'

'So can I come? Can Uncle Bill bring me, in his car?'

''Fraid not, darling. He's a bit too busy at his Works and London's an awfully long way from Villa Road. But listen, I'm going to be coming home with Mum very soon. She's a lot better already but she's just a bit weak. The hospital wants us to stay here for a few days, till she gets her strength up. But if you really *want* to come…'

'No. Wait a minute,' interrupted Sally. 'I'm thinking.'

'You do that, sunshine girl,' said Dad, and he hummed a little hum over the phone. He'd always said that people shouldn't be rushed, when they were thinking. He had to have very big thinks himself, about his difficult jigsaws and other things.

What Sally had suddenly started thinking about was the clock. It had to be ready for when Mum came back, not only ready but back in its old place, in their hall. This meant that Charlie and his helpers were going to have to work very quickly indeed. *But would there be enough time?*

'I think I won't come, Dad,' she told her father, 'if you really will be home soon.'

'Good girl,' he said, sounding relieved. 'But would you like to go to Auntie Pauline's house, till we get back?'

'No. It's all right. I'll stay here.'

'But you just said Mrs Spinks could be horrid.'

'Well, only sometimes. Anyway, I'm getting something special ready, for Mum, for when she comes back. All the things are here,' she added vaguely. Then she said, 'Dad, what do you mean by "a few days"? How long have I got left – I mean, to wait… ?' (Oops! She'd nearly let the cat out of the bag, about the clock.)

'Well, the doctor said ten days, but it could be sooner. Now until we do come home I'm going to ring you every night at six o'clock, at our house, and as soon as Mum is allowed to, she'll speak to you, too. Tell Mrs Spinks I'll be phoning her.' But at that moment Mrs Spinks came through the front door.

'I've told you not to use my telephone without my permission, Sally,' she began crossly.

'I didn't. It rang on its own and I picked it up. It's my Dad. He heard that Mum was very ill from a friend of mine, and then a doctor told him the same, and he jumped on a plane and came straight home from Abroad. I expect he'd like to talk to you.'

Sally gave the phone to Mrs Spinks and ran straight upstairs to her bedroom. She didn't want to hear her being all sugary sweet to Dad.

When she came down again Mrs Spinks had stopped talking to Dad, but she was still standing in the hall, staring into space. Her expression was a puzzle. Was it angry? Or only cross? Or did she just look embarrassed? Sally was still making up her mind about this when Mrs Spinks said in a tiny little voice, 'I'm sorry, Sally, I just didn't realise… I mean, about your mum. I thought I was doing everything for the best…' and suddenly she sank down on to the little chair that sat by the telephone and started to cry. 'If you want to go to your Auntie Pauline's you can go at once, I'll phone her now, this minute.'

All at once the horrid side of Mrs Spinks dribbled away. Now Sally could only think of the good things, how she'd taken Sally in at a minute's notice, because Auntie Pauline and Uncle Bill had gone away on holiday, how she'd cooked all those meals for her, even though they didn't taste very interesting, and washed all her clothes, and worried about her worrying about

Mum. And now she was sitting in a heap like this, sniffing and crying.

Sally patted her on the shoulder and found her a handkerchief. Mrs Spinks gave her a fresh one every single day, all beautifully ironed. She didn't approve of paper ones. That was another kind thing she'd done. Sally said, 'Mrs Spinks, I'm staying right here, till Mum and Dad come home. Of *course* I'm not going to Auntie Pauline's. Why should I?'

Mrs Spinks sniffed and blew her nose on the hanky. 'Well I just thought… your Daddy was a little bit sharp with me.'

'I'm sure it's because Mum's been so ill, Mrs Spinks,' said Sally. 'He can be sharp with me sometimes. He doesn't mean it.'

Mrs Spinks blew her nose, put Sally's handkerchief in her own pocket and said, 'I'll get you a clean hanky, dear. And here's your front door key. You can go home whenever you like. Your daddy will ring you tomorrow at six o'clock. Perhaps you'll be able to speak to your mummy, too.'

Sally wondered what on earth Dad could have said to Mrs Spinks because then she said, 'I've nothing in for tea and I don't feel up to going to the shops. Would you like fish and chips?'

'Yes *please*,' Sally replied. Fish and chips was her favourite meal.

So at half-past five Mrs Spinks gave her some money and a shopping bag. 'Here you are, then,' she said. 'Fish and chips twice and some mushy green peas. They'll have just started frying. It's always best to have the very first batch, before the fat gets those nasty bits and pieces in it.'

So, feeling a lot happier than she'd felt for ages, and also very hungry (as she'd never felt when she'd sat down to eat one of Mrs Spinks's grey dinners), Sally walked up to the Green Café which was on the corner of the next street but one.

She liked going to the chip shop. Mr Groarke, the owner of the Green Café, had a wonderful chip-making machine. Mrs Groarke peeled the potatoes and then Mr Groarke took one and put it firmly on some spikes. Then he pulled a handle down and out at the bottom, through some sharp square holes, fell wonderfully neat chips, into a bucket. Then, when the fat was piping hot, he put them in with a great sizzling sound.

While she was waiting for the chips to get crispy, Flossie the florist came in from her shop next door. 'Sally Bell,' she said, beaming down on her, 'I hardly recognised you, you're getting to be such a big girl, and you're the very person I was looking for. You've saved me a journey.'

'Have I?' said Sally. What on earth could Flossie the florist be talking about?

When the fish and chips were ready and wrapped up in three layers of newspaper, to keep them warm, and the peas in their little cardboard tub, she walked round to the flower shop.

Sally couldn't remember a time when Flossie's hadn't been there. She was quite old and rather plump. She wore lovely straw hats when she was arranging her flowers to sell, and long floating scarves, and she always smelled nice. She had a huge black cat called George and he had his own special cushion to sleep on, in the very middle of the window.

She gave Sally an enormous bunch of flowers, all beautifully arranged and tied with white and yellow ribbons. 'These are for Mrs Spinks,' she said. 'It was a special telephone order. Just came through. I thought I'd drop them off on my way home. But will you save me the trouble, dear? My old legs aren't too good today.'

So Sally slung the shopping bag over one arm and carried the flowers home very carefully. Who on earth could have sent such a big bouquet to Mrs Spinks? Did she have a secret boyfriend? Sally had thought the Bright Hour meetings were just for ladies. It was all very mysterious.

Mrs Spinks was ready for her, in the kitchen. The table had been laid and there were two plates warming on top of the stove. The minute Sally came through the door she put them on the table. But then Sally said, 'These flowers came for you, Mrs Spinks. Flossie at the shop asked me to bring them.'

'For *me*? Oh no, it's a mistake Sally. People don't send flowers to me, well, not any more,' she added in a sad little voice.

'But they are for you, look, here's a card with your name on.' And Sally gave it to her.

Mrs Spinks laid the flowers very carefully on to her draining board. Then she put her spectacles on, and read the card.

'Mrs Spinks… are you all right?' Sally asked, when she said nothing at all, but just went on staring at the little card, for ages and ages.

At last she handed the card to Sally. The message was from Dad. It said: 'Thank you for looking after Sally in our Alley'.

And then Mrs Spinks burst into tears *again*!

20

Next morning, when Sally woke up, the great big stone that had been lying across her chest for weeks and weeks, the stone that was about Mum being in hospital and the clock falling down, had gone. Instead of getting out of bed very slowly because she had to lift the horrible stone away first, or wriggle out from underneath it, she leapt to her feet in seconds. She felt brilliantly light and she wanted to skip around. She felt that if she ran down the street the littlest puff of wind might make her float away.

Mum was definitely getting better. Dad had said so. With luck, she would be able to speak to them both at six o'clock tonight. And in ten days' time (or even sooner... *help*!) Mum would be coming home to The Cedars. So it was absolutely vital, now, that Charlie Bates dropped all his other jobs and got on with mending Grandfather.

The minute she'd finished breakfast Sally went next door to her own home. After cleaning out William's cage and feeding him, she shut him in again. It was mean but there was such a lot to do. She just didn't have time to chase him round the house.

First she must phone the Buttons. She wanted to say thank you to Miss Button, for ringing Dad, and she wanted to get an urgent message to Charlie. But when she rang Appleford 616 nobody answered, not even Flo.

Sally hoped this was because Mr Button was much better and that Miss Button had taken him away on a little holiday. She had spoken of this plan. Flo could drive a car and they were going to hire one and ask her to take them to the seaside where Mr Button could practise walking up and down on his newly-mended hip. Perhaps at this very minute they were sitting looking at the sea, or listening to a band playing, down on the sands.

She went into her father's study and sat down at his great big desk. Then she took a piece of paper and wrote this letter:

Dear Mr and Miss Button,

I hope you are well. This is just to say that my mum is a whole lot better and coming home in ten days' time. Thank you for telling Dad. Charlie is getting on with the clock and I hope it is going to be ready, for when my parents get back.

Lots of love,

Sally x x x

Then she took a second piece of paper and wrote Dear Charlie but almost at once she realised that there wasn't enough time for notes.

The problem was that the Bateses had no telephone. There was nothing else for it, she would have to go and see Charlie in person and tell him that the clock must be ready just as soon as possible. But when she pulled her bicycle out of the shed, and started to push it along the garden path, the nasty jolty feel of it told her at once that it had got a flat tyre. She bent down to look and found a large rusty nail sticking out of the back wheel. With a sinking heart she put the bicycle away again. She didn't know how to mend punctures.

She walked up the garden into Mrs Spinks's vegetable patch where, on tall canes, sweet-peas were growing in rainbowy swirls of colour. The smell was honey-sweet and insects buzzed in and out of the glowing flowers. Perhaps, on the day Mum came home, Mrs Spinks would let her pick a bunch. Sally sat down on an old stool. It was so warm and quiet and sweet-smelling that she nearly fell asleep. But then she poked herself awake and decided to go back to Dad's study. It was always a good place to think, when she had a problem.

On the desk there was a little black notebook labelled Useful Phone Numbers. She opened it and saw that it was like an address book with a different page for each letter of the alphabet. Sally turned to 'D' and found three different things under 'Delivery Services'. One said 'Post Office', one said 'Broadfield Express Delivery', and one said 'Mr Moses, Butcher'.

Sally decided to try Fred at Mr Moses' shop. He might be out on his rounds or he might be sunning himself outside on the pavement. The number was Broadfield 577 and the operator lady put her through straight away. Fred answered, which was a relief because Mr Moses always looked a bit fierce, especially when he was sharpening his knives. He was a tall burly man with a long gingery beard and when he laughed he opened his mouth so wide you could see all the gold fillings in his teeth.

Fred said there was nothing much doing in the shop and that he could come at once. So Sally went back to the letter she'd started to Charlie.

Dear Mr Bates,

she began (now it was all so urgent she had decided the letter must sound as official as possible),

> My mother is a whole lot better and my father will *be* bringing her home from the hospital very soon so it is...

(what was the word Dad always used, when people were slow with things, and he got cross... oh yes)

> ...it is IMPERATIVE that the clock is ready just as soon as you can manage it. I am sorry to rush you. Please pay Fred out of the bag of silver and please let me know how the clock is getting on, Love Sally

Then, thinking that it might hurry things along, she added

> P. S. NO EXPENSE NEED BE SPARED.

She had just written Charlie's address on the envelope when the doorbell rang.

'Name of Sally Bell?' said Fred, with a wink. Then he looked down at the small white envelope which she had put into his hand. 'Is this all?' he said doubtfully.

'Yes, but it's extremely important.' Sally was feeling rather pleased with herself for having thought of using Fred, like Charlie did. But then he said, 'OK. Here's your bill. It's cash, isn't it?' And he held out his hand for the money.

Sally took a deep breath. 'Mr Bates will pay you, at the other end. He is looking after my money. It's all explained in my letter.'

But to her great surprise Fred gave her back the envelope, 'I'm really sorry, miss,' he said. 'But I have to be paid in advance. Those are my orders, from Mr Moses.'

'What does "in advance" mean?' asked Sally.

'It means that you have to pay me before I do the job, like, now.'

'I've just told you,' explained Sally. 'There is plenty of money to pay. It's just that Mr Bates has it. He's doing a big job for me. I've paid *him* in advance.'

The young man looked at her. 'How much in advance?'

'A hundred whole pounds,' Sally told him. 'As a matter of fact you brought the parcel with the money in yourself. That's what was inside it.' Then she had a thought. 'Do you know who sent it?'

'Can't say I do,' Fred answered. 'Bit of a mystery, that was, if I remember. Nobody knew – at least that's what the boss told me.'

'Well, will you take this letter to Mr Bates for me,

or not?' Sally said. Then something inside her suddenly grew rather hot and cross and she said, 'Listen, if you don't believe me, about Mr Bates having my money, I'll get another firm to take my letter. There are others I can ask, you know.' And she decided to shut the door. Everything felt terribly urgent now and Fred didn't seem to trust her. Sally didn't like that one bit.

'Wait on, miss, I'll speak to the boss,' he said. 'Can I use your phone?'

'Well, all right. Go through to the kitchen, it's in there.' And Sally opened the door again, to let him come in. While he was phoning she sat on the hall carpet and stared rather miserably at the long shadow on the wall, where the clock had been.

When Fred came back he looked a bit sheepish. 'Boss says it's OK, as it's Miss Bell. There's no charge, anyway... well, not to you, there isn't. My new instructions are to carry all your messages for free.'

'What do you mean?' Sally asked him. 'Your boss doesn't even know who I am. I just rang up.'

'Ah well, *you* don't know *us* but it seems *we* know *you*, and the boss says there are special instructions, on our books.'

'But I'm not on your "books",' Sally said in exasperation. She was getting more and more bewildered now.

It was Fred's turn to look puzzled. 'Sorry, miss, but

that's what the boss said. I reckon it's all to do with that parcel I fetched for you. Right mystery that was. Still, why look a gift horse in the mouth, that's what I say.'

Sally didn't understand this saying but she didn't want to spend time on it now, nor on thinking who on earth could have been speaking to Fred and Mr Moses about her troubles. It was probably a mistake. But just at that moment it felt like the most amazing good fortune, almost as amazing as the bag of money coming. She could use Fred to exchange letters with Charlie. That way he could keep her bang up to date on progress, and she could let him know the minute she knew when Mum and Dad were coming home.

Fred was holding out his hand for the letter. 'Sorry about the mistake, miss. I'll go right now, and I'll be back in two shakes of a donkey's tail, with any reply. You see if I'm not.' And he snatched the letter from her hand again and ran down the path to his bicycle. Sally wondered if he was telling the truth, it was all so amazing. So she called after him, 'Come back! If it's breaking the rules I'll ask somebody else.' But Fred had gone. She shrugged, closed the door properly now and walked slowly along the passage.

Sally decided to clean the kitchen. Mrs Spinks was talking about spring-cleaning the whole house before Mum and Dad came home. It didn't really need it but cleaning was one of Mrs Spinks's hobbies. Sally thought she'd make a start herself, just for something to do, but she'd only got as far as wiping down the tops and rubbing at the bits of the windows which she could reach, when the doorbell rang and it was Fred back again.

'I found Mr Bates, no trouble. And he's sent you a reply. Any message to go back, miss?' He smiled at her while she undid the envelope. He was still a bit of a puzzle. First he'd said he wouldn't go at all and now he was being so helpful.

> *Dear Miss Sally,* (Charlie had written.)
> *I will push all the boats out to do your job*
> *within the next ten days. There are a few*
> *tricky problems but never say die.*
> *Yours and obliged,*
> > *Charles Bates.*

'Any reply?' said Fred, his head cocked on one side, like a bird.

'Er... I don't think so. What does "push the boats out" mean?'

Fred scratched his head. 'I think... does it mean, "I'll pull out all the stops". You know, do my absolute best, like.'

'I expect that's it,' Sally answered. 'Yes, I'm sure that's what he means.' She wasn't at all sure, but it was important not to waste any more time.

'He's a grand old feller, your friend Charlie Bates,' said Fred enthusiastically.

'Yes he is.' Sally nodded.

'Are you sure there's no message to go back? It's no problem. Sky's the limit. That's what the boss said.'

'Are you certain about that?' Sally asked him cautiously. All these messages whizzing backwards and forwards were going to cost an awful lot of money.

'Those are my instructions.'

'Well, all right. Please tell Charlie that I'd like a progress report about my clock, every day, if it isn't too much trouble. I'd like you to collect it from Spodden Cottages at, er, five o'clock each day, and bring it to me. Is that all right?'

'Sure it's all right,' Fred answered. 'I've usually finished my meat deliveries by then. I'll go straight back now and tell him. No need to write it down.'

Sally went back to the kitchen and decided to scrub the table with some hot soapy water. There was rather too much buzzing round in her head now. She was so excited about Mum getting better but so worried about Grandfather not being ready in time that she wanted to do something really boring, to take her mind off everything.

Cleaning was the most boring thing there was, and the most disappointing because everything got dirty again so quickly. How could it be one of Mrs Spinks's hobbies?

21

At six o'clock that night, when the telephone rang, Sally heard her mother's voice for the first time in many weeks, for an eternity it seemed, when the moment came. The voice was quiet and a bit breathy and it said, 'Hello, darling, it's your old mum speaking. I'm dying to see you.'

Sally answered, 'You're not old.' (Mum wasn't, she was quite young, and very pretty.) It was a funny thing to have said, after so long, and she felt she must have sounded rather grumpy. But the words she really wanted to say wouldn't come out, there was such a huge feeling of gladness swelling up inside her heart, and suddenly she could feel tears running down her cheeks.

'Are you all right, darling?' Mum asked. 'Say something to me, sweetheart.'

But Sally couldn't, so there was a silence, Then she heard some sniffing and the clearing of a throat and she knew that her mother was crying too. It was the relief, that everything was going to be all right. It was just too much.

The next few days behaved just like the weather. It was all mixed up. One minute the sun was shining and the next it rained and inside Sally was feeling just the same. When the phone rang and it was Mum and Dad, to tell her things were improving every day, she felt happy. But then, when she read the latest report on the clock from Charlie, she felt anxious. It seemed to her that the mending was going much too slowly. She mustn't let Dad bring Mum home yet. She mustn't come back before Grandfather did.

'Dad says I'm making wonderful progress, Sally girl,' Mum told her, the second time she was allowed to talk on the phone, and Sally said, 'That's great, Mum.' But at the same time she was looking at a letter from Charlie Bates.

In his beautiful curly script he had written down exactly what was happening to Grandfather. It said things like *Solomon Biggs has started painting the little girls. Jim Tickle has carved new finial. Regret, broke. Is trying again. Self glued and cramped (five hours)*. Sally didn't really understand all this, nor exactly what the people with funny names were doing, nor what 'finial' meant, or 'cramped'; but Charlie had sent a drawing, showing how the mending was coming along. It looked as if Grandfather was still in an awful lot of bits. That night she lay awake worrying and when the morning came it felt as if she hadn't been to sleep at all. After breakfast she went next door and phoned Appleford 616. Miss Button would know how to hurry Charlie up, or how to delay Mum and Dad, but there was still no answer.

Mrs Spinks, having made certain sure that William was firmly in his cage, came in to The Cedars to begin her great spring-cleaning and Sally helped. They worked so hard, rubbing and scrubbing and dusting and polishing, that Mrs Spinks was exhausted by dinner time. 'No more cleaning today, Sally,' she said. 'After we've washed up I shall go upstairs and have forty winks.' This meant Sally could go home again, without feeling that Mrs Spinks was spying on her.

On the third night Mum and Dad phoned to say they'd be able to come home very soon. 'I want to see my little girl,' Mum said. 'I'm missing her.'

'I'm missing you too,' Sally told her, and this was true, only *Please,* she was saying to herself, all the time *don't get home before Grandfather does.*

'I'm thinner than I was,' Mum said. 'I didn't eat for ages, when I had the fever.'

'Perhaps you should let the hospital fatten you up a

bit?' Sally suggested. 'Before you come home.' But Mum said, 'No fear. I want some home cooking. I'm looking forward to fish and chips from Mr Groarke's, and to some of Mr Moses' pork sausages.'

When the phone call was over Sally opened the latest progress report from Charlie.

> *Glue drying nicely but we are still waiting for new springs. Couldn't get hold of Solomon Biggs, to see how the painting's getting on.*

'This is hopeless!' Sally said aloud. The new picture Charlie had drawn, of Grandfather's progress, didn't seem much different from the first one.

All glueing done he had written ('Well that's something,' Sally said to herself,) *waxing and polishing nearly completed* ('and that's good too,' Sally added) but then she read:

> *New fingers have to be made and, regret, workshop shut for the holidays. Solomon Biggs says no chance of finishing before the end of the month. Oh heck!*

'"Oh heck", *indeed*,' Sally said in such a loud voice that William, whom she'd let out to have some exercise in the kitchen, ran right along the workbench and shot up the wall where he sat on the round-faced clock.

'Oh no you don't,' she said, and, managing to catch him, she shut him back in his cage. 'None of this would have happened if you'd not taken to running up clocks.'

She was seriously worried now. Without the hands Grandfather would look very odd and wouldn't be able to tell the time, and he would look very naked and bare without the paintings. She reached to pick up the phone, to ask Fred to take an urgent message to Charlie, when it rang and it was Dad again. 'Wonderful news, Sally Sunshine,' he said. 'Mum's been given the all clear. We're coming home on Saturday.'

'*Saturday*?' shrieked Sally. 'That's, well, it's... marvellous.' But when the phone call was over she felt even more muddled. She longed to see Mum and Dad again but not before Grandfather was standing in the hall. Something terrible was going to happen if Mum got home before Grandfather. She'd had that hunch all along.

She would have to send a message to tell Charlie that Saturday was going to be Clock Day, but when the lady tried the number there was no answer. Mr Moses must have closed his shop, or be having forty winks. Grown-ups always seemed to be having forty winkses.

From Dad's study she got the little black book and looked up 'Taxi Services'. The first entry said 'A1 Taxi

Cabs' so she rang them at once and said, 'Please will you send a taxi to The Cedars, Villa Road. I have to go to Spodden Cottages, in Appleford. There and back. It's very urgent.' 'Rightio,' said a voice. And when the taxi man rang the doorbell ten minutes later it was Ron.

The minute Charlie opened his front door Sally started to talk. Everything came out in one big rush, Mum being miles better and coming home on Saturday, but how could they get the fingers made when the workshop was closed, and what had happened to Solomon Biggs who was painting the little girls and... and... 'Charlie,' she burst out 'It's just *got* to be finished.'

'Whoa, Miss Sally,' said Charlie. 'One thing at a time.'

'Who is it, Charlie?' Mrs Bates called out. Sally could hear the noise of a wireless set and could vaguely see the shape of someone sitting in an armchair.

'Just a clock enquiry, dear, it's Miss Bell. Good news, her mother's a whole lot better.'

'Well, that *is* good news,' said the shadowy Mrs Bates.

Charlie took Sally's hand. 'Dear Miss Sally,' he said in a very solemn voice, 'I will do all in my power to get your clock home by Saturday morning. I will use some of your money to do the rounds of all the places that just might have the bits we still need. I will chase up

Solomon and Cyril and Jim and tell them to get a move on. And what they cannot do I will do myself. If it's all done it'll be a bit of a miracle. But miracles do happen sometimes. So you are not to worry.'

'Thank you, Charlie,' she said, and she swallowed very hard. 'I'll have to pay the taxi man out of the bag of silver pennies.' But Charlie took some money out of his pocket. 'Here,' he said, 'pay him with this. I'll make a note of it. And don't worry, we've hardly touched your money yet.'

So Sally rode home in the taxi. When she thought of Charlie's cherry-red cheeks and his kind brown eyes she felt a lot better. She had some cocoa with Mrs Spinks, watched the television for a bit, then went upstairs. She felt very tired after what felt like rushing around all day, and worrying.

After she'd put her nightdress on, and cleaned her teeth, she sat on her bed in the dark. She hesitated for a minute, then said in as firm a voice as she could manage, 'Hello, God, it's me again. Thank you for letting Mum get better. It's wonderful. But the thing is now... well, it feels greedy asking for things all the time, but please, could you arrange it so that Charlie will finish the clock in time? He says that, if he does, it will be a bit of a miracle, so I thought I would ask you. Yours sincerely, Sally Bell. P.S. Thank you in advance, and Good Night.' As she fell asleep she wondered if

God ever got any actual sleep Himself. People were always awake somewhere in the world, asking for things. Mustn't He get very tired?

22

There were only four days to go. Sally was counting. Mrs Spinks, having spring-cleaned the house until it dazzled, had started work on the back garden. She said she wanted everything to be 'just perfect' for Mum. The thing was that Mum liked her garden a bit wild. She didn't mind a few weeds and nettles, they brought the butterflies. But Mrs Spinks wouldn't listen. 'Every weed must go!' she said grimly.

All this gardening meant that Sally could be in their house on her own. She always got nervous round about the time Fred was due, in case Mrs Spinks should see him and ask why the butcher's boy kept coming round. But by four o'clock she had usually gone home exhausted.

Then, on the last but one day, when Sally sat in the hall, waiting for a message from Charlie, Fred didn't come. She waited and waited for his bicycle to come rattling along the street but it never arrived. And when Mum and Dad rang, to say they were all set for Saturday and they'd be home by eleven o'clock in the morning, she began to panic. The next day was Friday.

This meant that Grandfather must be in place by tomorrow night. But was he ready yet?

AND WHAT ON EARTH WAS CHARLIE DOING?

She decided to ring Mr Moses but after the lady had tried it she said, 'Sorry Madam, but this number is out of order.' 'Oh *no!*' screeched Sally, banging the phone down.

All of a sudden, as if it rather minded this rough treatment, the phone started ringing, making hurt little bleeps, like an injured bird. 'Hello?' Sally said, picking it up.

'Hi Sal,' a voice replied. 'How are you doing?' It was her brother Alan.

'Alan! Where are you? You sound very near.'

'Well, I'm quite near,' he said, 'though there's a bit of water to cross first. I'm coming home. I've got some leave. I didn't know The Mum had been in hospital. The Dad just rang and told me.' Sally laughed. Alan always called them 'The Mum' and 'The Dad'.

'That's amazing,' she said. 'Will you be home tonight?'

'No, not till Saturday. My leave doesn't start till Friday midnight.'

'But couldn't you come a bit early?' said Sally. She was thinking, if Charlie had finished the clock, she and Alan could put it back in its place together. Alan would know how to keep Mrs Spinks out of the way.

But he said, 'Nope. Sorry Sal. They're very strict. But I'll definitely be home on Saturday, see if I'm not. Must dash now, there's a queue of blokes all waiting to use this phone.'

When he had rung off Sally felt very lonely and very helpless. She had fixed up the mending of Grandfather all on her own. And now all the people that could have helped her get him back home on time seemed to have gone silent, or be too far away to help. And it seemed that there was no way she get in touch with Charlie Bates. Had something awful happened to him? Had the cottage burned down? There must be some reason why he'd not sent his usual message with Fred. Though she didn't expect anybody to answer she decided to ring Appleford 616.

The phone rang and rang and Sally got gloomier and gloomier. She sat thinking about Mrs Button's house, about the long jungly drive to the blue front door with its creeping ivy, about the big fat goldfish plopping about in the sink. But just as she reached up to put the phone back on its rest, somebody picked it up, at the other end.

'Hello?' said a voice. The person was puffing and

very out of breath. 'Sorry to keep you waiting. This is the Button household but I'm afraid—'

'Flo,' Sally interrupted, 'it's me, it's Sally Bell.'

'Oh *hello*,' answered Flo. 'I was just thinking of you. Miss Button's still at the seaside, with Mr Godfrey. But there's a message here. "Very important" it says.'

'What does it say, Flo?' Sally said. 'Quickly, what does it say?'

'Er-um, er-um… oops… sorry… '

There was a silence. 'Flo?' Sally called down the telephone. Then, '*Flo?*' What on earth could she be doing?

'Sorry. Just needed to clean my specs… steamed up… there we are. Er-um, er-rum, now then it says, "Nearly there. Will deliver nine-thirty, Friday night. Usual place. Agnes will accompany. Signed, Charlie Bates".'

'Thank you, Flo,' said Sally, and as she spoke the words her voice felt terribly small and trembly. But was it true? 'Please will you read it again, Flo?' she asked. 'Just to be sure I've got it right. You see, there must be no mistake.'

So Flo repeated the message, saying the words extremely slowly. She sounded wonderful, Flo did.

'Thank you very much,' said Sally.

'That's OK. Any reply, if the party should ask for one?'

'Er. Just say, "message received and understood".'

'Will do. Anything else?'

'Yes. Please give my love to the Buttons.'

'Will do. They're as brown as nuts.'

Friday night came in a rush, and this time there was no problem about Mrs Spinks spying on them. She was tired out after all her cleaning and weeding. The Cedars looked marvellous. It was so clean and so tidy that Sally felt she hardly dare walk on the shiny floors, or sit on the settee, in case she squashed one of the beautifully plumped-up cushions.

In the hall, in Grandfather's place, a great vase of flowers stood on a table. These were the same flowers that Dad had sent to Mrs Spinks. She had said, 'Your Daddy won't be offended if I put them here for tomorrow, will he Sally? There's not much in my garden in the way of flowers, in August, except for the sweet peas of course. And it's such a wonderful bouquet he sent me.'

'I'm sure he won't mind, Mrs Spinks,' Sally told her.

'I hope you don't object to me saying so, but that table looks a lot better there than the old clock,' Mrs Spinks continued. 'Dust-traps, that's what all that fancy old furniture is, just dust-traps.'

'Mm…' Sally replied. She was already wondering how she was going to move the huge vase of flowers out of the way in the dark, without knocking it over.

At twenty-past nine that night she crept through the front door of Mrs Spinks's house. Through the hall ceiling and down the stairs came the sound of loud and regular snoring. Sally pulled the door shut behind her with a sigh of relief. Never again would she have to cover her ears with the pillow, to try to get to sleep. Never again would she have to eat grey dinners, or wash jam jars covered with cobwebs. Mum was better again and Sally was going home for ever and ever.

She had only just gone down the garden and out into The Backs when she heard a clopping noise. Her heart fluttered and she stood to attention by the back gate of The Cedars, peering into the shadows. And a minute later, round the corner, came Charlie Bates sitting on his little cart, with Agnes pulling it. On top of the cart, all covered up in clean white sheeting, were some bulky shapes. 'Grandfather,' Sally whispered into the dark, 'is it really you?'

'All done, Miss Sally,' Charlie said quietly. 'Let's get the old man inside, shall we?' He said it in a very matter of fact way, as if he'd just stuck a spout back on to a tea-pot.

'But Charlie,' Sally said, 'it feels like a miracle.'

Charlie laughed. 'You could say that. Didn't think we'd make it in time, me and the lads, but well – let's get it on with it, shall we?'

So Sally crept up the garden path and opened the kitchen door. This time, before letting Charlie in, she made very sure there was nothing he would trip over. It was all much too heavy for her to help with the carrying so she just walked at his side, and held doors open, and put the vase of flowers in a corner. After quite few trips all the separate pieces of the clock were standing in the hall, still covered with sheets.

For a minute, after several journeys up and down the path, Charlie stood and rested his arms. 'Are you all right, Charlie?' Sally said. 'Would you like a cup of tea? Mrs Spinks put some fresh milk in the pantry, for when Mum and Dad come home.'

'That would be very nice, Miss Sally,' Charlie said. 'But let's get our work done first, shall we?'

So while Sally watched, Charlie pulled off the sheets, one by one. Out of the gloom of the hall, which was only lit by a tiny lamp lest anybody passing by should see, emerged wonderful things: soft, glowing wood and polished glass, rich colours and shining brass. Every bit of the grandfather clock looked as good as new; in fact they all looked better than new.

Charlie carried the bottom part across the floor and set it in place, where the flowers had been. He knew exactly where it should go because there were grooves worn into the carpet. Not even Mrs Spinks had been able to get rid of them. When it was exactly right he carried the trunk across. This was the case in which the weights lived, and the pendulum, the case that had been split right in two, when the clock had crashed down. It looked perfect again to Sally. You couldn't see where it had been mended, not the tiniest line or crack. 'It looks fantastic, Charlie,' she whispered.

Next came a very important part, the part Charlie called 'the movement'. This meant the face of the clock, with all its complicated works tucked tidily behind it. 'See that?' Charlie said, 'Cyril took it to bits and cleaned it all up for you. It was really mucky this clock was,' and he showed Sally the working parts which were made of brass, all polished now and gleaming with oil.

He fixed 'the movement' on top of the trunk, stood back and inspected progress. 'There now, looks better, doesn't it?' Sally looked up at Grandfather's face. There were the four little girls, perfect again in their rich colours, and the hands which had bent and snapped were perfect too. There was the moon, just changing into the sun, and the months, and the days of the week.

'It still says July the second,' Sally said. 'It's August now.'

'Hold your horses, Miss Sally,' said Charlie. 'It's not time to set it going just yet. Listen, why don't you go and give Agnes an apple?' and he produced one from his pocket. 'And you could put the kettle on now. We won't be long finishing this.'

So Sally went off to see Agnes, and to find the tea things, and when she came back Charlie had hung the huge weights into the trunk and fixed the pendulum in place. He'd even wound the clock up and started it ticking. 'There now, are you pleased, Miss Sally?' he said.

Sally had a good look. 'Well, yes, but – er, haven't you forgotten something?'

Charlie frowned and pulled at his chin. 'I don't think so.'

But she knew that something was very wrong. Grandfather looked all undressed, or as if he had forgotten to put his hat on. 'It's the part which goes on *top* of everything,' Sally said, 'you know, the part which broke into all those pieces, the container that everything fits into. That part's missing.'

Charlie looked at her blankly, 'Oh, you mean the *hood*, the fancy casing with all the spiky bits? The part that was so badly damaged? Oh well, I'm afraid—'

'You mean it's not ready?' and Sally knew that she was going to cry.

Charlie's face broke into a cheeky smile. 'Of course it's ready, Miss Sally. I'm teasing you, that's all. Stand back,' and with a grand flourish, Charlie whipped a sheet off the only bit of clock that remained on the carpet. Suddenly, Sally didn't want to look, just in case it wasn't true, or in case they'd not been able to mend it properly.

'I'm not looking,' she said. 'Tell me when it's ready.'

She seemed to be standing in the dark for a long time. Charlie was talking to himself. 'Easy does it... a little bit this way... there now... that's champion.' She heard a whirring noise and then a series of clicks and *then* the grandfather clock struck ten times, and then just once.

'You can open your eyes now, Miss Sally,' Charlie said. Sally opened them.

'Oh, *Charlie...* ' she gasped and she crept forwards to join him. Together they looked at the clock. The 'hood' was in place now; Grandfather had his hat on. Every bit of carving was back: the pointy bits, the roses, the little wooden columns that stood on either side of the glass door, and you really couldn't see where it had all been mended. 'But there were so many pieces, Charlie,' Sally said. 'There were millions of pieces.'

'Ninety-seven,' Charlie corrected her. 'Well, I'm glad you're pleased, Miss Sally. The lads did a grand job, they more or less worked through the night.'

'And *you* did a grand job too,' Sally told him. 'But Charlie, something's different. At the top. It's not quite like it was. There was always a gap.'

'Ah, you've noticed have you? That's the bit I'm really pleased about.'

In the very middle of Grandfather's 'hood', where there'd always been a plain bit of wood, and something obviously missing, there was now a third carved rose with carved wooden petals and a stalk with tiny thorns. 'That's how it would have been in the olden days,' Charlie told her. 'One of my clock books had a carved hood with roses on it. It's just how yours would have been.'

'I wonder who made this clock?' said Sally.

'Isaac Adams,' Charlie replied. 'A man called Isaac Adams made it, in 1832. The name and the date have been engraved inside, but you can't see them, unless we take it to pieces again, and we don't want to do that, now do we?'

'Isaac Adams,' repeated Sally to herself, as Charlie cleared up and she went to make the tea. One day she might tell Mum about Isaac Adams.

While he was drinking his second cup of tea Charlie glanced at his watch. 'My goodness me, Miss Sally, it's eleven o'clock,' and at that very moment Grandfather struck eleven times, as if he'd heard. 'I must get off home now.'

'But you'll be in touch, won't you Charlie?' Sally said. She very much wanted to give him a little hug, just to say thank you, but she didn't like to. He might not be a huggy sort of person.

'Now this here,' said Charlie, in his official, clock-mending voice, 'is what I have not spent, from the bag of silver,' and he gave Sally a thick brown envelope. Inside you will find a diary of the clock-mending, and what everything has cost.'

'I don't want it,' said Sally. 'You can't give me all this back, Charlie. It doesn't feel as if you've used any, hardly. It's still quite heavy.'

'Of course you must take it, Miss Sally, fair's fair. I've spent what I had to. Now you look after it. Put it away in that nice leather bag, for a rainy day. And the minute your daddy comes home, you get him to screw Grandfather to the wall again; properly, mind.'

'I promise,' said Sally and five minutes later, with his dust sheets neatly folded up and back on the cart, Charlie drove Agnes away again, down along the back of the houses.

She waited until the clop-clopping had died away, feeling happy and sad and excited and nervous, all at the same time. Then she did a very bold thing. She went back inside her own house, and up her own stairs, set her own alarm clock for seven o'clock so she could get back to Mrs Spinks's for breakfast the next morning, and slept in her very own room.

23

Mum and Dad came home at ten minutes to eleven the next day. Sally knew the exact time because she checked with Grandfather before she opened the door. His beautiful, newly-painted face told her also that it was the twenty second day of August. She heard herself say, 'You've been away so long, Mum,' and the next minute she was in her mother's arms.

The hug lasted a very long time, so long that in the end Dad said in a hurt little voice, 'What about me?' and a voice behind *him* said, 'And what about me?' and when Sally peeped over Mum's shoulder, there was Alan, all smart in his army uniform with his black boots polished so shiny Sally could almost see her face in them.

After that, everybody hugged everybody else and it was only after quite a time that Mum, who had sat down on a chair in the hall, said, 'The house looks wonderful, Sally. Who's been spring-cleaning?'

'Mrs Spinks,' she explained. 'She's spring-cleaned the garden too. She never stops cleaning things. It's her main hobby.'

'Where is Mrs Spinks?' Dad said, 'We must say thank you. We've brought her a present.'

'She wouldn't come with me,' Sally said. 'She said it was just family, Mum coming home and everything.'

Mum had started looking round. 'I've really missed Grandfather,' she said. 'All they have in hospitals are little round electric clocks. They don't even tick, let alone chime the hour. They have to be silent.' Then she took a long look at the clock. 'He looks very, very shiny, Sally,' she said. 'Has Mrs Spinks been polishing him too? It looks as if the hands have been polished as well. How on earth did she do all this?'

Sally was beginning to feel a tiny bit uncomfortable. 'She didn't. It was… I sort of… climbed up.'

'You mean *you* did all this cleaning? You climbed up there all by yourself? Oh, Sally, you could have had an accident.'

Dad was now inspecting the clock very carefully. He said, pointing up at the face, 'Sally, there's something different about this clock. It's not just the polishing.'

'Is there?' she said, trying to sound very bright and breezy. 'What do you mean?'

'There's something different up, at the top, only my forgettery's not working. Mum, can you remember how it was?'

Mum got up from her chair and had another long look at Grandfather. 'Yes,' she said very slowly, 'I can remember. There was always a gap at the top, where a lovely carving should have been. And now... there *is* a lovely carving. There's a wonderful big rose, between the two little roses.'

Sally said, coming up from behind and taking hold of her mother's hand, 'Jim Tickle carved it. Charlie said that's how it must have been, in the olden days, when Isaac Adams first made the clock.'

'Sally,' Mum said, 'am I dreaming? Who are all these people?'

'The people who mended it, the people who mended Grandfather, Charlie Bates and Jim Tickle and Solomon Biggs and Cyril Jenkins.'

'But the clock didn't need mending, Sal. It was quite all right when I left it, well, not all beautiful like this, but it was certainly going.'

'It stopped,' Sally told her. 'It stopped the day you went into hospital and I climbed up to wind it for you, and it fell over. And it broke into millions of pieces. So I just *had* to get it mended, didn't I?'

Now she had told them the truth Sally was feeling wobbly again, so she sat down on the floor. And instead of going into the kitchen and sitting down at the table, to ask her to explain herself, The Mum and The Dad and The Alan all sat down beside her very close, and snuggled up to listen, and as she told her story the grandfather clock ticked gently away, looking after them all.

'One thing worries me, Sal old girl,' Dad said at last. 'It's Charlie Bates's bill. It'll be enormous.'

'There's nothing to worry about, Dad,' Sally told him. 'A bag of money came, a bag of half crowns. Charlie didn't even need it all. There's lots left. It was a miracle.'

But Mum seemed not to be listening. She was looking at her clock again. 'Do you know, Sal,' she said, 'I'd been feeling ill for quite a long time, long before I went to the hospital. I didn't tell anyone.'

'You should have,' said the others.

'Yes, I know. But I didn't. Anyway, it's only now I'm properly better that I realise how nasty I'd been feeling. And that's what you've done for Grandfather, isn't it? After being all broken, by the accident, he's been made, you know, even better than he was before.'

'Well,' Sally said. 'It was one of my hunches. I just knew that he had to be mended before you came home. You both had to be mended.'

'Sally,' said her mother, wrapping her arms around her, 'you really are the most amazing daughter, not just in this street, or in this town, but in the entire world.'

'I second that,' said Dad.

And Alan said, 'I third it.'

And everybody hugged everybody else, all over again.

The Saturday before school began again there was a party at The Cedars. Sally chose the guests and made a list of them (in no special order) in her best writing:

Guest List

Charlie Bates and Mrs Bates
Mr Godfrey Button and Miss Arabella Button
Mrs Spinks
Flossie the Florist
Linda Smellie and the two young Smellies
Solomon Biggs
Cyril Jenkins
Jim Tickle
Fred and Mr Moses
Flo
Agnes the donkey
Ron the taxi man

Every single person agreed to come and Agnes was happy, because it was a fine day so the party could be held in the garden. It was a party to thank everybody who had helped to get Grandfather mended, whether they knew they had helped or not. People like Fred and Ron said they'd just been 'doing their job', but Sally told them that they'd still been helping.

Miss Button talked to Dad, about when he was a little boy at her school, and then he talked to Charlie and Jim Tickle and Cyril Jenkins and Solomon Biggs, about mending the clock and about how he loved old things too.

Martin Smellie fell into the pond and Alan fished him out and Edward Smellie cried a lot, but stopped when Sally sang to him. Both the Smellies had a little ride on Agnes and then Sally had a big ride, right along The Backs.

Mrs Spinks went round with plates of food, including some cakes she'd made herself, but they weren't grey, they had pink and white icing. Mr Moses brought some sausage rolls made from his own sausages and Flossie the Florist had put little posies of flowers everywhere, including one in Agnes's straw hat. But the straw hat fell off in the end, and Agnes ate the posy.

Everyone had dressed prettily, or smartly. Mr Button's beard seemed to have grown even longer now. It had got much bushier and made him look more like

God than ever. Miss Button looked the very prettiest in a swirling dress of rainbow colours and a feathery hat, and when she swirled anywhere near Sally there was a smell of something lovely, something sweet and spicy that reminded her of something else, though she couldn't remember what.

At the end they all drank a toast to Sally. They raised their glasses, or their teacups, and said, 'Well done, Sally, for mending her mummy's clock, all on her own!'

'Well, getting it mended,' Sally whispered to Charlie, because she was always truthful.

It was a wonderful party and everybody kept telling her how amazing she had been, and how clever, and how 'resourceful'. But there was one important person who should have been there and whom Sally couldn't invite because she was such a vanishing person. It was Amber.

Not until Christmas time, when the Fair came back, did Sally see Amber again, and then they went down to their old place, to the stream at the end of the allotments, where they had their important talks. It was crispy cold now and the brown stream was covered with ice and they were both wrapped up in thick windcheaters and wore scarves and boots and gloves.

Sally told Amber about the clock falling down, and

breaking, and how she had phoned Appleford 616, to see if she could speak to God. 'And did you?' Amber said, her brilliant dark eyes flashing, 'Did you speak to Him?'

'No,' said Sally. 'A lady called Miss Button answered instead. It was her brother Godfrey I saw, in the end. His friends used to call him 'God'. It was just a joke. They helped me though. I'd have never found Charlie Bates without them, or all the other people who helped.'

But Amber had already lost interest. 'So you didn't actually talk to God then?'

'No. But there were miracles, you know, sort of magic things.'

'What kind of magic things?' said Amber, perking up.

'Well, a bag of silver came in a parcel, to pay for the clock. Nobody knew who had sent it. And a lady who has no money at all gave a whole ten shillings, and that helped. Then a person paid for all the messages to go to Charlie and back to me. They paid Fred who does the deliveries at Mr Moses' shop. Nobody knew who it was.'

'Could have been anybody,' said Amber rather scornfully.

Sally didn't reply. But she suddenly remembered the lovely spicy smell which had wafted out of the leather bag that had contained the silver coins and how she'd smelled that smell at her party, when Miss Button floated by in all her rainbow colours.

'Well it must have been somebody,' she said at last. 'And anyhow, it doesn't mean it wasn't a miracle. Does it?'

'The thing is,' persisted Amber, throwing a pebble on to the brown ice and watching it skate across the stream, 'did you actually see anything? I mean, did you actually see God?'

Sally was silent for a minute. Then she said what Miss Button and Mr Button and Charlie had said to her, when she had asked them the same question. 'Not exactly.'

But even as the words came out, she felt that she had.